Published by 4Radiance Publishing House
ISBN: 9798672771502

God, Joe Palooka, Dad and me

The fist photo on the cover is of the Joe Palooka statue in the center of downtown Oolitic, Indiana. Joe was the title character in a popular newspaper comic which ran from 1930-1984. He was a gentle and kind-hearted boxer. In his stories, he was often quoted as saying, "I'll only fight against crooks an' bullies."

Joe Palooka was a favorite comic character of my father's back during World War II. In fact, my dad had been bullied when he was young. He learned to box and that is when his bullying situation changed. My dad went on to be a boxer in the Golden Gloves for several years before starting his family. He continued to read Joe Palooka for as long as a local newspaper carried the comic and shared his love of comics with me.

When I began being bullied, my father tried to teach me how to box, in order to stop the bullying. However, Sunday school teachers taught us follow Jesus' words to turn the other cheek. This created a dilemma for me as a kid. Do I do what my dad wanted and fight back or do I follow Jesus and not fight?

Ultimately, I would choose to follow Jesus (as far as I understood His words at that time). This was not the easy way out of that situation. The bullying went on for around 10 years. Even though there were scary moments, each time a bullying situation felt dangerous, God provided a way out for me time after time.

While I struggled with the names they called me for many years after, the path of following Jesus proved to be the perfect release from all the pain I went through. And, in the end, that struggle became the inspiration for this novel.

I discovered this Joe Palooka statue during my father's later years, when he had dementia. It was my desire to take him down to visit the statue at some point, but his health declined rapidly after that. Since then, I have visited the statue a couple more times. It reminds of my dad in his boxing days, of Joe Palooka and when he would say, "Thank you, God," for getting him through a difficult situation.

Dear Reader,

Having been bullied in public school for more than 10 years, I know the struggles a bullied person faces in life. Even though my bullying ended in high school, its affects went for decades afterward. I had been called names hundreds of times growing up and I had begun to believe them. The names I had been called became little recordings in my mind. So, for years, whenever I failed at something on my first try, a little voice in my head said, "loser." Any attempt and failure at anything made me feel the bullies were right. Why even try anymore?

Likewise, whenever I felt any type of fear, I'd hear "sissy" in my head. From this I developed anxiety attacks. This just felt like I was having more fear. The more it happened, the more I'd hear "sissy." The more I heard it, the more it seemed to be true. And I had nothing to fight the voice in my head saying "loser" or "sissy" with.

These struggles led to serious depression in my life. And there were many times I didn't want to go on living. After all, the Bible said God would send cowards to hell. Coward was just another word for sissy. I must be letting God down too. There was no way He would allow me into heaven.

Ironically, it was God who held the answer. While seeking a deeper relationship with Him, He taught me new definitions for bravery and masculinity. What I had been believing were lies. Over time, He gave me a new vision for who I was and a new path to follow. My entire life changed. The depression lifted.

That is the heart in which I wrote this novel. Yes, it is a fictional story, but one written from experience. It is my hope through the story of Jan Richards, those being bullied will feel encouraged and the eyes of many others will be opened to the seriousness of this issue. God does care about it. And, more importantly, He cares about you.

Kurt J. Kolka
Grayling, MI

Acknowledgements

Diane Kolka

Rebekah Kolka

Gloria Penwell-Holtzlander

Jen Gentry

Sarah J.R. Smith

Samantha Fury

John Elderidge

Cindy Sproles

Rev. Steve Datema

Rev. David Longstaff

Janine Tacey

Julie-Allison Ieron

D.A. Reed

Jeff Kersten

Rick Norwood

R. Robert Pollack

Randy Erickson

The Staff at the

Devereaux Memorial Crawford County Library

… for providing research material and information

Teachers who allowed us to imagine being storytellers ...

Robert Woodland, Michael Delp and Garry Barrow

Prof. Robert C. Campbell, Prof. Sherry Beck

(Concordia University – Ann Arbor)

and Dr. Sandra Lovely

(Former English professor at Anderson University – Indiana)

wherever you are

Contents

Afraid We Are Not

Dedication

To those of us who have struggled with the demon of bullying; to those who love a victim of bullying and may have even lost them; to those who don't understand; and to those whose words cause more pain than any fist ever could, may this story touch your hearts.

Afraid We Are Not

Prologue

(Summer 1969)

His body tore through the prickly branches of bushes. They ripped at his bare arms and cheek. The only sound he was sure he was hearing was his own breathing and footfalls upon the forest trail. Yet, he was quite sure he could hear more footsteps behind him, getting closer.

To his right was the steep hill leading to the school track and the adjacent elementary school. To his left, a mix of white and red pines and cedar trees. Large ferns hid the ground and whatever slithered beneath them. Thick black muck guarded access to the gentle river beyond. His only hope seemed to be to reach the top of the hill at the end of the trail and come out where there were houses again.

He looked back. No sign of anyone following, but the sandy trail was ever curving, obscuring his view. He just knew he was being pursued. If he stopped, he was dead.

Nine-year-old Jan Richards rushed down the pathway at top speed. He knew he wasn't real fast, but what else could he do? His tennis shoes kicked up sand and golden-red pine needles off the foot trail as he dashed ahead.

His windpipe was becoming a dust bin, picking up all sorts of dust and pollen. That meant one thing. His asthma would soon be kicking in.

"Sissy-boy, you're dead meat!"

The voice of Mark Fury sounded closer now. He must be gaining on him.

Keep going! Keep going! Jan told himself. You can do this. You really can. Little faster. Just a little. The path should start going up just ahead. After that were houses and people. Grown-ups.

Jan gritted his teeth to squeeze out just a little more speed. Mark might catch up while he was charging up the hill. It was harder running uphill. Don't look back. Run. Run!

Then, just as he felt like he might be gaining a little more speed, the thick root of a white pine grabbed his foot. It sent him tumbling to his left toward the forest.

As he struck the ground to the left on his shoulder, he crashed through ferns and rolled over to a fallen tree before stopping. Now, the wheezing started. Jan clamped his left hand over his mouth to suppress the noise. That's when the other voice kicked in.

That was so stupid! Why didn't you watch where you were going?

His left shoulder ached from striking the ground. At least, he didn't land in the muck. The dirt was still solid here. Pushing himself back against the tree, he kept low. Ferns, the white pine and a cedar tree hid him from the path.

Then came the thunder of footfalls upon the sandy trail. Mark Fury blazed by with eyes set straight ahead. Within a few seconds, Jan couldn't even hear Mark's footsteps any longer.

Tripping and falling out of sight was not the manliest thing to do. Yet, it seemed a better ending than what might have been with Mark on his trail.

Jan shoved his right hand into his pants pocket. At the bottom was the cylindrical object he needed. Removing the inhaler, he quickly took two puffs. They left a bad aftertaste but would get him breathing regularly again.

Slowly and soundlessly, he picked himself up out of the black dirt and little green plants which were shooting out around him. All was silent except for the river flowing over rocks and branches about fifteen feet away. Jan felt something prickly against his neck all of a sudden. His left hand reached back around to the other side of his head. Pine needles.

He pulled them out of his hair and looked at them. Had he not felt them, he probably wouldn't have noticed them. Their color was similar to his own light red hair. The needles were just a little softer in color.

Slipping the inhaler back into his pocket, he stepped forward and peered through some tree branches. As far as he could see, the path stood empty as it came to its next curve. Nothing in sight. No sounds. He appeared to be alone with the squirrels and birds. Waiting just a few more minutes, he made his way up the hill to safety.

* * * * *

That night, Jan came out of his bedroom in his pajamas. His shoulder just ached a little from his fall on the path earlier. He peered around the lamp sitting on the side table next to his doorway. His parents sat at the far end of the light blue living room talking in hushed tones.

"I still think it's too bad about that Quarry boy," his mom said.

"Yeah. But he always was a bit of an oddball," said dad.

"That doesn't make it any less sad," Marge added. "He just graduated a year ago. He had his whole life ahead of him. What would make him do that?"

"Like I said, he was an oddball. Remember he worked at the flower shop."

"Oh, what does that have to do with anything?"

"It tells you he wasn't quite a normal boy."

"Oh, you men."

Jan stepped out into the open.

"Well, there's my little man," Mom said.

"On his way to becoming a big man," Dad added.

He ran over to his auburn-haired mom who wrapped her arms

3

tightly around him. Then backing her head up, she began assaulting him with kisses all around his face. "But you'll always be momma's boy, won't you?"

"Now, cut that out. Jan's going to be a tough guy. Too much mushy stuff weakens the muscles. Come here," said his dad grinning widely as he sat on the couch in a pair of dark pants and undershirt. In its rolled sleeve, the undershirt held tight to a cigarette pack like a cowboy's holster holding a six-shooter. His dad's black, close-cropped, hair made him look so strong and tough. His mustache lined up perfectly with the edges of his lip.

Jan and his dad shook hands. His dad's paw-like hand swallowed Jan's in its grasp but shook it gently. Dad grinned again and gave him a quick wink. It made Jan's heart jump when he did that.

He looked down at the newspaper pile at his dad's feet. "Dad, can I …?

"Read them one more time? Sure."

"But just once more," Mom said.

"You will, right, son?"

Jan smiled.

"A boy has to have his adventures," Dad winked again.

"You men."

Jan scooped up the newspaper comics section off the floor and ran off toward his bedroom. Leaping onto his bed, he turned on the night light and peeled back the pages until he found "Dick Tracy" and "The Phantom."

As he read through the strips once more, he could hear his parents talking in hushed voices again.

"Ya gotta stop babying that boy, Marge. Too much cuddling ain't good for boys. All this protecting him all the time, while I'm gone, has got to stop. Do you want him to turn out to be a sissy?"

"Oh, now you're exaggerating, Sam. Stop it."

"The world is rough on boys. They've gotta be tough to make it."

"The world is rough on everyone."

"You don't know what's expected of boys, Marge. There are

things he has to get through in this life that girls don't. Expectations. He's gotta know he's got what it takes."

"What it takes for what, Sam?"

"I can't explain it to a woman. You wouldn't understand. But I want Jan to be a real man!"

"I've never met a boy yet who turned out to be a woman."

"A sissy."

Jan pulled the comics section away from his face and pressed the illustrations of heroes against his chest and began rubbing them over his heart.

"If you want him a certain way, why don't you spend more time with him?"

"You're the one that wants Sue to go to college. How're we gonna do that unless I work every moment I get? I'm not having our kids go through what my family went through. Our kids are gonna have a better life."

"That was thirty years ago. The world is different now. And I'm not having Sue miss this opportunity to better herself."

"Well, I just want our son to be a real man, Marge. He's gotta learn to be tough!"

From his bedroom, Jan stared at the comic section against his chest. Even in hushed tones, their words carried underneath his bedroom door. He knew sissies were boys who were girl-like. He just wasn't sure what all that meant.

His dad made it sound like boys could become girls. How did that happen? Did too many hugs from moms make a boy's private parts shrink up, leaving them looking like girls?

Jan sure hadn't been tough today. If his dad knew he hadn't fought back against Mark Fury, it probably would have made him mad. Boys were supposed to fight. It was in every western and Tarzan movie they ever watched together.

Even in the Bible, God sometimes told people to go to war. That meant fighting. And God told men to be brave and strong.

And yet … Jan's Sunday school teacher, Mrs. Beach, had told his class about how Jesus wanted boys to "turn the other cheek" because fighting didn't show others God's love.

That made no sense. A boy couldn't be a brave fighter and a sissy. Jan flung the comics section down on the floor.

To be honest, Jan never felt brave when Mark or some of the other boys were around. He felt terrified. Name-calling challenges to fight fired from their lips. What would his dad think if he knew how Jan felt?

Do you want him to turn out to be a sissy? A sissy.

The negative voice echoed his dad's voice in his head. Maybe his dad thought he was becoming one already. Mark Fury said he already was one. His dad was definitely angry about Jan becoming one. If God wanted men to be strong and brave, He must really hate sissies too. Was God ashamed of Jan for running from bullies? Would God leave him? Does He walk away and not come back at some point? Jan began to feel tears run down his cheeks.

Only sissies cry.

I don't want to be a sissy. But what if I can't help it? Jan wondered. His whole body shook at the words in his head.

That's when his stomach started to churn. There was a sharp pain too. He squeezed his eyes shut and gritted his teeth. Arms hugged his abdomen. He wanted to call for his mom. But after what his dad said, he didn't want them to see him not being able to handle a little stomach pain. So, he rolled over onto his stomach. It would be better to keep this a secret too. It was probably something only sissies get.

Chapter 1

(Mid-January 1976)

W hen his mom called him the second time, Jan peeled himself up off of the white sheets and moaned. Everything in him told him to lay back down and cover his head with his blanket. He had hoped for a snow day.

Propping himself upon his knees, he peeked out the window next to his bed. Wind blew the heavy snow in waves, sometimes veiling the house next door. A snowplow rushed by, hurling a white quilt atop sidewalks already sleeping beneath previous blankets.

Obviously, the school superintendent believed the TV weatherman's forecast of the storm ending by noon. Down in Detroit, school would have been called off last night. Here in Northern Michigan, snowstorms were common and to be expected. Schools were called off only for the very windiest days and greatest accumulations at one time.

Winters could be harsh and long-lasting, especially here in Gunwale, on the AuSable River, snuggled in the Snow Belt Region. Residents thought this environment was good for toughening people up. Especially children. So toughness training was held annually from

November to April.

"Gunwale is no place for sissies," people often said. Jan wondered where they went when they left here.

Jan turned from the window and looked down at his body, covered only by a pair of white briefs. It had a soft, fleshy appearance, which in no way embodied toughness. Rather, it seemed to Jan to be more girlish than manlike.

For a moment he stretched out his arm and examined it. Thin and soft, it looked more like a piece of modeling clay rolled too many times on a table. His hands carried on the small and thin theme. Even the hair on his arms and legs appeared more fine than coarse. Although the tufts of red hair from his armpits gave a small hope of masculinity someday appearing.

Jan could remember his dad's huge hands. They were wide paws with thick fingers with lots of callouses. His arms and legs were thick and well-defined from days running track in high school and college. Photos Jan had seen from his dad's teenage years reminded him of the old Tarzan movie actor, Johnny Weissmuller, but with a crew cut and a mustache.

Jan's arm dropped down in disgrace, his thin fingers brushing across the white cotton material of his briefs, as they fell to his side again. Jan looked at his soft, undefined form and the cotton veil. He breathed a deep sigh. Somehow, in some way, his body looked like it had stalled in its attempt at puberty. His 15-year-old classmates all stood taller and bore more hair, as far as he could tell.

"Jan, are you up yet?" His mother's voice pierced the wall from the kitchen.

"Yeah." Jan plodded over to his dresser and began picking out clothes. His mother's voice lowered, but he could still hear her talking with Sue.

"You know Jan," his sister said. "He's probably daydreaming again. I swear he should have been born a girl. Dress him up in pink and no one would know the difference."

"That'll be enough of that talk, Sue."

8

"It's true, Mom. Most guys are into sports or cars or hunting. He just hides in his room doodling."

Jan pulled open his sock drawer. A baseball rolled around in the back as he pulled out a pair of colored socks. Quickly, he pushed other socks back to surround the ball to keep it from rolling around and making noise. Closing that drawer, he began opening others to pick out the rest of his attire.

"Jan is quiet and polite. He'll make someone a fine husband someday."

"The way he's going, he'll more likely be the wife."

"Sue!"

"I'm going. I'm going."

The outside door slammed, and the kitchen grew quiet.

Jan plodded back through the thick, brown shag carpeting where he dropped his clothes onto his bed. He picked a comic book up off the floor beside it. His fingers flipped through the pages one last time. Surely, staying home and rereading the adventures of The Phantom would be preferable to going to school. Or anything else for that matter.

The art in test issue was by a new guy named Don Newton, who used lots of dark shadows in his artwork to make the Phantom more mysterious. Page one of the comic book read "The Beasts of Madam Kahn." A former circus performer, Madam Kahn, had come into the jungle nation of Bangalla with a group of thugs who bore resemblances to various members of the cat family. Her mission had been to deceive the Dusaambasi tribesmen, who worshipped animals, into going to war with other tribes. Her goal was to eventually take over the recently-independent Bangalla government through a rebellion by the tribes. Of course, she hadn't reckoned with …

"Jan! I don't hear that shower running."

"I'm going!" he shouted.

Placing the comic on his nightstand next to a black-covered Bible, he scooped up his bathrobe. Jan covered his body fully, pulling his robe tightly around his neck. He dashed to the small bathroom located in the void between his and his parents' bedrooms. The door locked as it shut.

By the time Jan had showered and was back in his bedroom, his mom had left for work. He quickly snatched up the pair of bell-bottom jeans and a new shirt. It was one of the kinds of shirts with a zipper partway down the chest and a ring pull. He loved it.

Jan walked out through the living room into the kitchen and plopped himself down at the table. A bowl, spoon, an already-filled juice glass, cereal boxes, and pill bottles made a half-moon around his spot. He poured the frosted corn flakes into the bowl, folded his hands, and said a prayer.

Next, he shook some pills out of their containers into his palm. The pills were different shapes, but all dull colors. Kind of like the walls in their house. Light, dull colors. Each time Jan looked at them he was reminded of that week when he was twelve and he first had to take them.

Jan had been in the hospital for digestive issues at the time. Every day was another test to find what was causing Jan's stomach pain. Many included sticking tubes or objects into his butt. Even worse than the pain, however, seemed to be the pain it caused his dad. As long as his dad stayed in the hospital room, he constantly fidgeted and appeared to be in pain himself. He hardly looked at Jan. With every test given, his dad left the room for a long smoke, sometimes not returning for hours.

After several days of testing, their doctor declared Jan had a chronic intestinal disease. They could control it with medication, but he'd have it for the rest of his life. There would be some limitations too. The doctor told them the disease may flare up occasionally, especially in times of stress. Depression was a possible issue. Jan would likely tire easily after physical activity. High school sports would not likely be in his future. Jan breathed a sigh of relief.

But then, he looked over at his dad. Dad's bright eyes went dull and shot a long, hard look at the floor. After that, Jan couldn't remember Dad looking directly at him again.

The next day, during deer hunting season, his dad was found dead in the woods. The sheriff and coroner, who had been close friends with his dad as kids, declared it a hunting accident. The funeral and everything happened so fast. It seemed a blur now.

The first time Jan remembered taking his pills was the morning of his father's funeral. Something about the dull color of the pills reminded him of his dad's eyes when the brightness went away. They both seemed lifeless.

Water pooled in Jan's eyes as he swallowed the pills with his orange juice. They tasted bitter. With milk on his cereal, he munched away, staring at the tiger on the cereal box. Now, the house seemed empty, even when he, his mom and sister were there together. Jan felt lost.

Chapter 2

Quickly, Jan slipped on his green winter coat and walked toward the door. Now came the first of several hurdles for the day in the life game he called dodging the bullies.

He peaked out the backdoor window. A few kids were making their way through the curtains of snow, squeezing the bottom of their hoods tightly together. They appeared to be mostly middle-schoolers and teenage girls. That was probably a good sign.

Still, the feeling of uncertainty lingered. He walked back to his room for a minute. Everything looked so peacefully there. He wanted to return to bed and grab his Phantom comic book. The thought made him look back at his nightstand where the comic sat waiting. Next to the comic, his Bible held out a folded piece of paper.

He walked over and slipped out the typed page. It was a shortlist of bible verses Pastor Enoch had asked the youth group to read throughout this week. Today's verse was Psalm 13.

Jan wasn't big on reading his bible, even though he knew he was supposed to. Comics always felt so much more exciting. However, the pastor always reminded the youth group faith required growth. Growth only happened through reading the Scriptures.

Someday he would get better at that. He was sure that's what God would want too. Someday. But, before that Jan would have to change some things. God wouldn't want a sissy trying to get close to Him.

He looked out the window at the swirling snow outside. Kids were walking past, but he couldn't tell who they were. Well, he thought, reading a bible verse would use up more time. He turned to Psalm 13 and read the first few verses.

How long, Lord? Will you forget me forever?
How long will you hide your face from me?
How long must I wrestle with my thoughts
and day after day have sorrow in my heart?
How long will my enemy triumph over me?
Look on me and answer, Lord my God.
Give light to my eyes, or I will sleep in death,
and my enemy will say, "I have overcome him,"
and my foes will rejoice when I fall.

Instead of providing answers, God's words seemed to be mocking Jan's feelings. The words seemed like Jan's own thoughts on most days. Except Jan's thought didn't sound so eloquent. The eloquence, however, didn't make the words any less depressing. What did the writer mean by "I will sleep in death"? Was he afraid of being murdered in his sleep or was he depressed and contemplating suicide? If those were the only two choices for a sissy, he'd rather not think about it. So, he closed the cover without finishing the Psalm and walked back out into the kitchen.

Where was God these days? Jan wondered. It seemed in bible times, He was constantly making Himself known to those who believed in Him. But where was He when Jan was at school? Where was He when the bullies came around? Maybe God only did want tough guys in His presence. Guys who were never afraid. Real men.

Between cold bursts, Jan looked out the window at Mark Fury's house. Why did the Bible have to remind him of his enemy? All appeared dark and quiet there at the brightly-colored Fury house. With any luck, Mark had already left for school. The start of this day might be promising after all. Zipping his coat up tighter around his neck, the fifteen-year-old stepped out into the harsh world. It almost looked like Gunwale was being consumed by the snowstorm. Drifts had begun to swallow up the streets and sidewalks. Some sought to swallow even houses but were not yet high enough. It looked like winter's version of "The Blob." He wished Mark Fury would get swallowed up by it. Suddenly Jan pictured a giant snowball rolling down the street with only Mark's head and hands protruding from it. Jan snickered for a moment.

Callously, the arctic wind woke him back to reality. It stung his ears, turning them blood red. In Gunwale, it was against the guy rules to wear the hood on his coat. Guys needed to be tougher than a little wind. He could have worn a knit hat, but that might make him a victim for a game of keep-away at school.

The wind teased his carrot-colored hair and its bitter cold stung his eyes, making them water. He drew his hand up to his face, acting like he was blocking the pummeling wind and snow. Then, after using all his peripheral vision while not moving his head, Jan used his gloves in quick, intentional motions to wipe some fleeing tears. He wondered if neighbors were staring out their windows.

Soon, Jan knocked on the door of Steve Reddy's house. Immediately, his tall, dark-haired, long-time friend stepped out the doorway.

"'Bout time you got here, Richards. Another minute and I'd have left without you."

"Oh, well," Jan replied with a grin.

"'Oh, well,'" Steve mocked jokingly. "Sometimes I think those are the only words you know." Steve punched Jan lightly on the shoulder.

They tramped off the porch into the January blizzard.

Jan had known Steve since before first grade. Their morning ritual of going to school together started out pretty much the same on most days.

"I got a letter from Mindy on Saturday," Steve said.

"Ooo ... the other woman. What did she say?"

Mindy was a girl whose grandparents lived next to Steve's grandparents' place outside of town. She lived downstate somewhere in the Detroit area but came up to visit her grandparents occasionally on weekends. Steve made sure he was always visiting his grandparents when she did. They'd go on long walks down the forest trails together and make out.

"She might be up next month. And she might bring a friend with her if you catch my drift."

"A friend?"

"A girlfriend, Richards. And her girlfriend might want to double-date."

"Meaning?"

"Don't be dense. It would be your chance to prove what a man you are." Steve scratched the thick hair under his nose. The mustache gave Steve the appearance of a rugged cowboy from a magazine cigarette ad.

"You just need a little more confidence, Jan. Being with a girl changes everything for a guy. You just wait and see."

"So, does Jenny suspect anything?"

"Are you kidding? I'd be dead if she did!"

"One of these days, you're gonna get caught."

"Nah. I'm too good."

They stopped briefly at the main street running through the center of town, Bateau Avenue, to check for traffic. Down the road to the right lay the elementary school and hospital. To their left, just a couple blocks sat the downtown area where the business loop off the freeway met Bateau Avenue. Retail stores gathered there at one of the town's three stoplights from which they spread out, mostly along the business loop.

Reacting to a break in the traffic, they crossed over and began their trek to the middle school, just a couple blocks ahead. Steve breathed in the cold air as if it were some freshly baked cookies from out of the oven. His mom did bake great cookies, but Jan simply couldn't wait until winter was over.

Suddenly, a car turned off Bateau Avenue and whipped past them.

"Jan, look!" Steve shouted. "That one's got one of the new license plates!"

The new Michigan license plates had flag-like images to them in celebration of the nation's bicentennial. The left quarter was dark blue with stars running down the side, except for the very bottom which had the number 76 in bright white. The rest of the plate was red with white letters and numbers. At the very bottom, there were flowing white stripes.

"When I get my license in the spring, I'm going to get my own car. It'll be blue and decked out with a flag on the antenna. You wait!"

Everyone seemed to be looking forward to the new year and the big celebration coming that summer. News commentators were preaching that America was finally coming out of its recession. That made the year look even brighter.

It was also an election year. President Ford would be challenged for his position come November, after having had it handed to him when Richard Nixon left after the Watergate scandal.

Jan and Steve trudged their way up to the middle school through the waves of snow where they met Jenny, bundled in a yellow parka and scarf, coming from another direction. Her blond hair waved behind her like a bridal veil beneath her white, knit hat. Together they hopped the next bus out to the new high school, a couple miles outside of town.

School districts had recently started a new tradition building high schools away from the downtown areas. Too many kids had been leaving the school at lunchtime and not returning for afternoon classes. Schools built out in the boonies appeared to solve the issue. Skipping, after all, was an academic felony which fit just below quitting school in the minds of school board members.

Time passed quickly on the bus as Steve and Jenny chatted amid the babble of other voices and the loud, hissing bus noises. Jan relaxed, leaning forward in the seat behind them. He listened to their conversation while mostly staring out the window.

As the pack of students trotted off the bus and into Gunwale High School, Jan stayed shoulder-to-shoulder with Steve and Jenny. Tossing coats, scarfs, and what-not in their lockers, they walked off down the hallway to pick up their class schedules for the second half of their sophomore year. Just like everyone else. A new semester, a new start.

Through the crowded, mustard yellow hallways supporting dark green lockers, they passed by clumps of students who were comparing schedules. Jan felt thankful he didn't see either Mark Fury or the "Weasel," another bully, out in the open. Around the school, office gathered tables manned by the two counselors and a few teachers handing out schedules by class and in alphabetical order. The three of them were given their schedules without much delay.

As they walked, they passed by Mr. Grace's room. Jan had always felt sorry for Mr. Grace. Some football players made it a rite of passage to frustrate him so much during class, he would begin to cry. English teachers MacEthain, DePlume, and Forrest stood in a room together talking about fishing. In the library, Mrs. Praats leaned over the counter and chatted with Mrs. McPhail as students returned their borrowed books to the student library assistants who checked the books back in. Guys and girls gathered beside lockers in pairs or groups; others rambled through the halls. One of the school's smarter kids, Eddie Bright, hurried by Jan and his friends. Upon his back, someone had taped a piece of notebook paper reading, "Kick me." Jan looked away in anticipation of what lie ahead for Eddie and moved closer to Steve as the three walked along.

Down at the far end of the hall, a group of seniors were playing keep-away with a freshman's knit hat. They had grabbed it from him and were tossing the hat back and forth to each other out of the freshman's reach. When they tired of the game, they would throw it up on top on a trophy case, or something tall, where the freshman couldn't reach it. He would then have to either give it up as a lost cause or seek help, in great humility, from some adult who would then make a comment about him being more of a man and not letting the seniors do that to him.

Jan looked down his schedule again. The toughest part of a new semester was figuring out where the rooms for each class were. Being sophomores, they knew who most of the teachers were and the rooms where they were usually found. Occasionally, however, one teacher would need to switch rooms with another teacher. And what could be more embarrassing than walking into the wrong room on the first day of class?

Jan went with Steve and Jenny to the door of her first-hour class. After a lingering kiss of 52 seconds, she unwillingly departed. Steve and Jan took off together, splitting up as Jan found the door into his first hour class.

Jan stepped into the cement block room with artificial heat and its painted light yellow facade. All eyes in the room seemed to shoot over to him expectantly as he entered. At the sight of him, however, they all look down in disappointment. He spotted some of the athletes, their round, hard muscles stretching their tight flannel shirts. He could feel the smallness of his body again. His arms felt limp and weak. They could beat him to a pulp at the slightest hint of fear.

Keeping a straight mouth and adding a concentrated look to his eyebrows, Jan walked toward the far side of the room. He spotted an empty desk behind Barry Lancer, a guy who was in his youth group at church. They nodded to each other with knowing grins. Jan slid into the seat. He had dodged his bullies in the walk to school and while roaming the hallways before school. Only seven more times this day would he have to be on his guard moving around.

Barry stood over six foot. He was lean but well-muscled. No one would ever consider messing with him. And his light brown hair came out in waves, giving him a sailor-like appearance. A lot of girls admitted to liking him.

The final students wandered in and took seats around him. Some were in his class. Others were juniors. A couple might be seniors who missed their history credit earlier by taking extra gym classes. None of the faces looked too threatening so far. His shoulders finally loosen up and he leaned back against the cool metal chairs exhaling.

This was Modern U.S. History. Not the most exciting class, however, it rated better than some of the other classes coming up that day. Gym would be the worst. It was the cesspool of school life as far as Jan was concerned. No one could tell or cared how you did in other classes. Gym however was different. In front of everyone, the activities showed "what you were made of," as his dad had often said. Or used to say. Before the accident happened.

Jan wasn't sure exactly what he was made of, but it seemed more fragile than the other guys. He would never even come close to what his dad had been. It was as if God, as a chef, had used a totally different recipe for Jan. Or maybe Jan just never rose up in the oven as God's other recipes did.

Something was obviously wrong. And Pastor always said, "God never makes mistakes." If that was true, only one person could be to blame for how Jan was turning out.

Monotone history teacher Mr. Gray now opened his attendance book. Quickly he called off the names of everyone who was supposed to be in the class. Students responded in annoyed mumblings. No sooner had he finished when the intercom on the wall screeched to life. The principal gave his usual welcome back for second-semester speech. That's when Jan's mind basically switched off.

To the right of Jan, Jill Peere and Karen Eibull whispered wide-eyed over the contents of a "Playgirl" magazine concealed in a notebook. He could see the well-muscled icon on the page with his thick mustache and hairy chest. The man proudly showed off his nakedness, displaying it like a fisherman with a prize catch. Jill traced the man's muscles with her index finger. She silently mouthed some ooos and ahs, looking up at the ceiling as if in ecstasy. Karen giggled and followed suit. The girls then looked around the room at the guys surrounding them. They seemed to whisper back and forth like judges at a bodybuilding contest. Suddenly, their eyes fell upon Jan. He was sure they had x-rays coming out of their eyes like Supergirl. A sharp chill passed through Jan. His body felt even smaller and more fragile. No doubt they could tell all he lacked in masculinity. Smiling at each other, Karen whispered a comment to Jill. They laughed in silence and turned back to the fine example of masculinity on the printed page.

Sissy-boy, the negative voice returned in his head. *Sissy!* Jan winced and tried turning his attention elsewhere. It might go away.

Jan turned his eyes toward other parts of the room. No one seemed to be listening. One group of juniors talked over some upcoming basketball games. Barry and the guy in front of him chatted about what they had been catching for the season while ice fishing. In the far back, some couples talked about taking a winter canoe trip down the AuSable River on the weekend. The thought of that made Jan shiver. One girlfriend ran her fingers down the grooves between her boyfriend's muscles on his back, showing through the tight shirt. The other girl clasped her small hands firmly around her guy's cantaloupe biceps.

On the other side of the room, Anna Enfold and Paul Buschall talked about the upcoming spring musical. They were both very talented in singing, music, and dance. In fact, they seemed like the perfect couple, yet they never displayed any affection in public. (Unlike Steve and Jenny.) Their relationship seemed to always make other students wonder if they were really a couple or not.

Jan felt a little jealous. Even though Paul liked drama club (a questionable activity for a real guy), he had Anna constantly hanging out with him. And only real guys had girlfriends, of course. Jan doubted anyone questioned Paul's manhood.

Meanwhile, Mr. Gray hardly seemed to notice no one was paying attention. Or maybe he didn't care. He was too busy looking over his notes on his desk. The principal's voice was soon replaced by one of the student office helpers, who giggled occasionally as she read the day's announcements. Jan took out his notebook and began sketching a skull to bide his time.

Announcements never affected him. He wasn't into sports or any of the other activities provided by the school. And there were no groups associated with art. Of course. Sports made money for the school; art shows did not. That's the way administrators and school board members thought. They were probably right. Most guys preferred sports over art shows. They all seemed to think art was for sissies.

Behind Jan, two upper-classmen, wrestlers, kept talking away.

"Coach wants me to gain another 5 pounds for Saturday's meet."

"Another five?"

"Yeah, he wants me to take on Nowak from St. Ignace."

"You think you can?"

"I think so. Coach is pretty sure I can."

"Nowak is the state leader in that weight category."

"Yeah, and I'd be in really good standing for state competition. Coach says if I take Nowak, it'll put me in the school record books for sure."

"You would be the manliest man among men in the whole state."

"Hey, it's my senior year. What better way to make my mark than to show Nowak who the real man is."

Real man.

Jan shrank down into his seat as the negative voice repeated the words over and over. The echoing word made it hard to concentrate. Each time he heard the word in his head, he could feel something like a needle pierce his heart.

You're never going to be a real man, it taunted him.

His small hands trembled on the desktop. Jan slipped them underneath and began running his hands up and down his denim pant legs. The material felt rough and strong against his fingers. Sometimes feeling something physical made the voice fade. He kept telling himself to think of something. Anything.

Suddenly, Mr. Gray began to speak. Jan focused in on the teacher's mouth and each word coming out of it. He told himself to concentrate, stay focused.

Mr. Gray began talking about the importance of this year being the bicentennial. Apparently the announcements had ended at some point. No one noticed. He talked about some special projects he wanted the class to work on. Then, in mid-sentence, he was cut off by the intercom coming back on with an added message.

"Will Jan Richards please report to the counseling office?"

Jan's eyes grew wide.

Now, what?! He couldn't help but wonder. He had gotten caught up on all his work from last semester and managed to pass his classes. Did he do something else wrong? Were they going to change his schedule?

Continuing to feel chilled, he picked up his notebook and walked toward the door. A deep voice followed him with a quiet shout out from somewhere in the back.

"Go get 'em, Jannie girl." Laughter trailed behind.

Sissy-boy. Sissy-boy has a sissy name.

"Quiet," said Mr. Gray in a raised, deeper tone.

Even the negative voice appeared to obey the command this time.

Jan hated his name too. Few others were more girlish sounding. However, his mom had insisted on the name after his birth. Supposedly she had gotten it from some good-looking Hollywood celebrity from her teenage years. She thought it sounded gentlemanly and affluent.

His mind turned back to the problem at hand. Getting called to either the principal's or counselor's office was never good. The only reason he had ever been called to either was because of his grades.

His weak stomach began to gurgle and churn. He took some deep breaths. The last thing he needed was another stomach episode now.

Sissies are weak everywhere.

The linoleum tiles on the floor were large off-white pieces with little drops of color on them forming a colorful chaos. His tennis shoes made squeaking sounds as he scuffled along. They echoed in front and behind him. Sometimes it sounded like the walls whispered in the midst of the echoes, "Sissy. Sissy." Even the building itself seemed to mock him.

Chapter 3

Jan opened the door to the counseling office and stood face to face with the familiar secretary. His heartbeat like a drum in a rock song.

"Hello, Jan Richards," she said in his usual, quiet tone.

"Hi," he muttered back.

"You're here to see Mr. Guideron, aren't you? Please step into his office there on the right. He'll be with you in a moment."

Jan obeyed immediately. Inside he planted himself on a small comfortable seat near the door and slid his notebook beneath it. There he waited. Before him was a large, dark, oak desk covered with folders and a bunch of papers. The walls, like those in the classrooms, were made of cold cement block but painted a bright yellow. From these hung framed degrees from a large university.

At last, a tall blond man in a polyester suit entered, closed the door and seated himself behind the dark desk. He picked up a folder and opened it.

"Well, Jan, you really brought your grades up at the end of last semester. I am very impressed by your hard work You must have worked on your focusing in class."

"Thank you," said Jan staring at the floor. He leaned back in the chair, his hands folded and his legs tightly together. Again, his fingers pressed against his denim jeans moving back and forth.

Mr. Guideron picked up another sheet of paper from Jan's folder. "Let's see. You have quite a mix of classes this semester. Which ones are you looking forward to?"

"Uh, drawing. I really like art."

"Really? I have a good friend in Chicago who's an artist. He does a lot of freelance work for publishing companies. He does quite well for himself at that."

"I have an aunt who's an artist. Mom has one of her paintings hanging in our living room at home."

"Maybe you have acquired some of her artistic talents."

"I don't think so. I'm not that good." Again, a pause. "My dad always used to say I had his legs. He ran track here when he was my age. Won some trophies."

"Are you trying to say you might like to try out for the track team?"

"No. I'm not good at stuff like that. I don't have what it takes." His fingers rubbed harder against the dark blue denim.

"That's right. You had some problems in Phys. ed., didn't you? The coach said you didn't like to participate. And you weren't taking showers."

Jan leaned farther forward, shrugging his shoulders, and stared at the green carpeting. He couldn't bear to look Mr. Guideron in the eyes when he mentioned that. His hands clenched the bell bottom of his jeans with all their might. Don't talk about that, his mind pleaded.

"Does your doctor know what is causing these episodes when you get really sick?"

"He says he is not sure."

"During Christmas break, I did a little research on your illness to better understand it. One article said that these episodes can be caused by stress." He paused briefly, then said, "Jan, is everything going well at home?"

"Yeah," he whispered.

"What about school? Is everything okay here? Sometimes there are problems going on with students that the teachers and administrators don't know about. They can affect a student's performance in classroom."

Jan shook his head slightly. He couldn't bear to look Mr. Guideron in the eyes. Stop. Please, stop, he thought.

The counselor sat back for a moment, looking up at the ceiling.

"Okay. When it comes to classes like gym, your best course of action, Jan, is to do what you are told to do. Don't worry about the outcome or how your best compares with someone else's. Make sure you participate at your best level. That's all. Then go to your art class and throw yourself into it. This school doesn't expect every student to be a trophy-winning athlete."

"Sure." Jan nodded his head, still not looking at the counselor.

He felt the counselor's eyes on him, however. Jan wasn't sure if he was awaiting more of an answer or if he was studying him for some other reason. Again there was a pause.

Finally, Mr. Guideron spoke again. "Jan, why don't you scoot your chair over here. Let's look at your schedule together and talk about these classes your taking."

For the rest of the hour, they talked about the classes. The counselor kept asking questions about how Jan felt about his classes. All Jan could think of saying was "okay." Mr. Guideron seemed to want more from him. What did he want Jan to say? He hated school? He hated his classes? Some of the other kids scared him?

The counselor concluded with, "My office is always open. If you're having any problems with anything, let me know. I'd like to help."

Jan picked up his notebook and walked out. The bell rang as he stepped into the hall. He still felt cold inside. His arms tingled. Then, he felt another sensation.

He walked quickly to the right, away from his next class. Back toward the gym, near the trophy cases, there was a small set of restrooms which weren't used as much as the others. They were mostly used by the public during basketball games.

Jan slipped inside. Only two other guys were inside but they were already washing their hands. He placed his notebook on one of the unused sink countertops and walked up to one of the urinals breathing out a sigh of relief. As he stood there, Jan heard footsteps behind him as the other two walked away from the sinks, toward the door. Then the door opened, allowing them out, and attempted to shut, but suddenly stopped it. Someone else had grabbed it to come in.

There was a tromp of new shoes, squeaky ones, coming closer. Then it happened. He heard the flick of a finger and immediately felt the sting against his ear.

"Sissy-boy, you came back," said the piercing voice of Mark Fury. "Too bad."

Mark bumped into him as he came up to the urinal immediately next to him and assumed the position. Jan could feel Mark staring at him through the corners of his narrowed eyes. The bully's voice became like a whisper. "You're lucky we're not outside right now. I'd kick your butt all the way back to town, sissy – just to watch you cry some more."

Jan ignored the comment and continued staring downward. His stomach began churning. It was starting. He knew this would be another bad day. Then, Mark glanced over at Jan's urinal and a sly grin came over his face.

"Sissies always have the smallest ones, Jan."

Mark turned back and stared down at his own urinal.

"No girl is ever gonna want you," Mark added, grinning at himself.

Jan felt his soul shrink inside. It wasn't the first time Mark had made such a comment since the gym showers began in seventh grade. The words made his soul curl up into a ball.

Mark quickly zipped up and turned away from the urinal. He walked briefly over to the sink, picked up Jan's notebook and thrust it into the trash can.

"Bye, Sissy-boy," came another whisper. Then came the tromp of shoes, straight out the door.

Outwardly, Jan stood still like a statue. Mark's words had frozen him in place. Bodily functions ceased. All Jan could do was stare and stand motionless. His mouth felt dusty and dry. There was no way to respond to a comment like that. Mark had been ahead of most other guys in developing physically. Even now, as other classmates had finished their development, Mark remained noticeably above average. In locker rooms, a manly body gave a guy the right to say what he wanted, because other guys always stood in awe of the most mature boys. Unless someone challenged him. Of course, no one would. There were plenty of signs on Mark's body of fights he'd been in. Obviously, he always won, because he always had stories to go with each of his scars. They were his trophies.

For young teenage guys, bodies were absolute proof of masculinity – especially in gym. In elementary school, what you could do in front of other guys used to be the proof. Now that was just the icing on the cake. Real men always looked a certain way. Tough.

And every guy knew what the physical signs of being a sissy were – scrawny bodies, lack of body hair, lack of muscles, small male parts. Jan's body shamefully dragged that evidence into the locker room every day, while Mark's showcased his trophies. No one could deny his manliness.

Sissies deserved to be harassed. Most guys seemed to think that way. There must be something wrong with them to not turn out the way they were expected. Rejects of evolution, some said. A curse from God for having fears, Jan thought. That had to be it.

Sissy. Sissy-boy.

The words kept echoing in Jan's head. He wanted to just collapse on to the cold floor. But that would really make him look like a sissy. Water pooled at the bottom of his eyes lids.

Just don't think about it, he told himself. Look up at the ceiling. Swallow. Let the tears flow back inside. You can control this.

The negative voice seemed to agree.

Yeah, you walk out like this and they'll know for sure you're a sissy. You don't need anyone else to leave you because of what you are.

Jan took some deep breaths. As the weight of the water on his eyes lessened, he grabbed his notebook from the trash and walked out of the restroom. Or, at least, his body walked out. His soul remained in hiding and pain dribbled down its face.

Chapter 4

It was the truth. All the bullies had to do was smack Jan once with their words, their name-calling, and his mind would make a recording of it. His mind then went on replay for the rest of the day. Or even longer. Each time the words repeated, his stomach would churn.

Jan stared blankly at his paper in his notebook the rest of the day, his stomach bubbling and churning. He must have made a trip to the restroom during every class. The diarrhea was constant and urgent in its need to leave his body. It seemed to take all its strength with it. With each trip to the boys room, he felt weaker. By noon, he was almost exhausted.

In classes, teachers talked away, but the meaning of their words became lost. Sometimes his hand grabbed his pen and wrote a few words. Fortunately, even in gym, the coach just talked about what he expected of students. No activities to perform.

At lunch, he was on his own. This semester Steve and Jenny had a different lunch period from him. There were other guys in his class who seemed nice, but he couldn't always trust who they sat next to. Some of the more zealous athletes would ignore Jan one day, but tease him the next. The other problem was most guys talked about sports or hunting, which Jan knew little about. If he sat next to girls, some guys would tease him about being one of the girls when they saw him in another class later in the day.

Finally, Jan spotted someone reading a book to sit next to. Readers made the best pretend friends. They neither talked nor expected him to talk to them. He could stay there as long as he wanted, so long as he remained silent. By now, the negative voice in his head had stopped talking. Unfortunately his brain had shut down as well. Likewise, his emotions felt totally absent. But he was safe.

Somehow, he made his way back on to the bus at 3:30. He couldn't remember who he sat with. His eyes stared out the window but recorded nothing. The walk home was equally memorable. Icy winds stung his ears red again.

Once inside his house, he threw his school books on his desk and made one more trip to the bathroom before collapsing onto his bed. For a moment he just lay there, taking a very deep breath, blowing out his cold sadness and breathing in some warm, safe air. Lying down usually made his digestive system settle down too.

Jan lay on his stomach, his hands grabbing the edges of the twin bed. Then, he closed his eyes. The blanket felt warm and soft against him. He wished the bed were not so wide or flat though. And maybe had a heartbeat. His cheek pressed against the soft pillow. It was a common experience being in that spot. Sometimes, he held onto the bed for long periods of time. But only when no one was around.

A tear ran down Jan's face again now. The scene from the restroom this morning came back into his memory. Mark's words kept repeating themselves in his head. Then, he heard his dad's voice: *I want Jan to be a real man. He's gotta learn to be tough.*

Sissy. You are such a sissy. The negative voice followed it, enhancing the point.

Jan hated the negative voice, but it always seemed to be right. He knew sissies always cried. And Mark was right too. Sissies had skinny, awkward, fragile bodies. Every TV show he had ever watched showed sissies that way. The way guys talked at school backed that idea up too.

What had made him so different from other guys he went to school with? Was there something he was supposed to do when he was younger? Where had the mistake been made? All he knew was that something every other guy had was missing from him. He just didn't know how to find it. Was he doomed to always be this way? His fingers gripped the sides of the bed tighter and he closed his eyes.

The outside of him kind of looked like a teenager or, at least, on its way to becoming one. But the process seemed to take forever on him. He hardly noticed any progress with his physical development anymore. As far as he could tell, his body didn't appear much older than 13. Deep inside, he still felt like a little boy. Small and helpless. What did God think of him now? He was probably ashamed too.

Most days fear was all Jan felt when he was around other guys. That had to make God angry.

His room grew darker as the winter sun lowered itself toward the horizon. From the dull, tan walls hung posters of singers John Denver and Jim Croce. A couple portraits of comic strip characters clipped from newspaper pages like Dondi and Gasoline Alley had been taped to the wall also.

Among these iconic figures stood some of his drawings he had tacked up to the bland wallpaper. He liked to take photographs of family members from downstate and make large drawings of them in pen. Some looked more like the real relatives than others, of course. There was just something about art which made him feel good.

His eyes would see something. His brain just seemed to translate reality into art and send the image out to his hand. From that point on, he had to draw what his brain had come up with. Art wasn't a hobby for him like it was for some people. It was who he was. The way some people talk as soon as a thought pops into their head, that is how art worked with Jan. It had to come out. Images would press on his mind until he couldn't stand it anymore. It was like going to the bathroom. He could only hold it for so long.

At last, from the bed, his eyes came to rest on the grim face of the Phantom on the wall. Jan had created the painting of his hero in

31

fluorescent paint from the dime store. When he turned out the other lights and turned on his black light, the painted images glowed while the unpainted background turned black, bringing his painting to life in the darkness. The bright neon colors gave the Phantom a mysterious appearance against the black background.

In the comics, the Phantom traveled the world, battling international criminals, pirates, corrupt businessmen and poachers. He was tall and muscular in his form-fitting, dark purple costume. The costume was purple because its material was dyed with berries from his secret headquarters in the jungles of Bangalla. The suit matched the berries creating the perfect camouflage in the jungle during the day. And its darkness made him blend into the shadows at night. Jan had learned about the reason for the color purple in a Sunday newspaper story last year.

The Phantom never felt fear. The villains feared him. And with his right fist, he left his mark on the face of evil-doers. The sign of the skull! It came from a ring he wore. Once marked by the Phantom, the bad guy would live out his life as a marked man. No one would trust him again. Jan's dad had read the Phantom, and many other comics, as a boy. The full-color Sunday sections had been a treat during the Great Depression. When Jan was about five, his dad came home one night with a Phantom model kit. They put it together and painted it. Actually, his dad did all the work. But even watching by his side felt wonderful.

As the scene faded from his mind, Jan heard the squeak of car brakes outside. Peeking around the corner of his doorway, he could see out the living room window. The newspaper delivery person drove up and stuck the newspaper into the box by the street. It had come early today. He quickly slipped on his shoes and threw on his coat. Dashing out, he snatched the newspaper from the box and ran back inside. Tossing his coat in the closet and kicking off his shoes again, he settled down onto the tan couch.

A quick check of the index box of the front page, Jan threw the unimportant sections on the floor and began to finger through the section he wanted. At last, he opened to page D6. There they were —

pages of art, words, and excitement. All anxiety began to fade and his stomach seemed to calm more as he entered the illustrated world.

The Phantom was tracking down the Star of Bangalla. A poor farmer had found the huge diamond while plowing in his field. When thugs learned of it, they beat him up and locked him in an old building. His granddaughter, learning of this, ran for help. In the jungle, she was found by the Phantom, who rescued her grandfather. Today, the Phantom approached the Blue Dragon bar, where thugs hung out, in search of information on the thieves who stole the giant diamond.

Jan knew what would happen next. That scene had played out before in other stories. Disguised in his trench coat, hat, and dark glasses, the Phantom would enter the bar. He would order a glass of milk from the bartender. The others in the bar would harass him about it and a brawl would break out. In the end, the Phantom (the only one standing) would leave the bar and walk out with the information he needed. The Phantom never started a fight, but he wouldn't let others push him around either.

Farther down the comics page, "Brenda Starr, Reporter" had just married her longtime boyfriend, Basil St. John, the mystery man, and adventurer. Seemed like they've been a couple like forever. Jan's dad had once told him Basil first met Brenda when he rescued her from a fire in December of 1945. Basil was one of those tragic figures in the comics. The men in his family had some terrible disease which drove them insane. He had to receive some serum derived from black orchids down in South America every so often to keep himself sane. On Thursday, they were finally pronounced man and wife before an audience of millions of readers.

One cool thing with the wedding was the cartoonist, Dale Messick, had asked readers to participate in the preparations. She asked them to design wedding dresses for Brenda. The winning design was used in the strip. Every once in a while, a cartoonist would do something like that to connect with readers.

Of course, Jan kept the fact he read Brenda a secret. Not even Steve knew that Jan read a comic about a girl every day. His dad sure

33

thought it was okay though. Sometimes, his dad talked about other girl strips he read as a kid like "Tilly the Toiler" and "Connie" which weren't around anymore. Then, there was "Joe Palooka," one of his dad's favorites from childhood which the area newspaper no longer carried.

Next, Jan turned to "Gasoline Alley." It was a comic strip about life in a small town. Although it was a humor strip, it continued from day to day like Brenda. His dad said the strip was older than he was. In fact, Jan's grandfather read it when he was young.

Just before Christmas in the strip, the town's spinster, Miss Melba, who was a cleaning lady, had gotten a promotion at the city hall. Now, she worked on the top floor. Well, the other cleaning ladies didn't like her, because she made them look bad. She actually spent her time cleaning. So, the other women, Bet and Berta, started causing trouble for her. They left big grease marks on doors "accidentally" and put ink in her cleaning solution. One time they locked her in the women's room while she was cleaning because she wouldn't leave 20 minutes early like they did. That was where the funny part really started though.

While cleaning the underside of the restroom sink, her hand bumped into something soft and papery. Down came $600 in cash on the floor. Being the sweet person she was, Miss Melba turned the money over to the City Hall people. No one claimed it, so it became hers.

Imagine, finding that kind of money, while cleaning! If Jan thought he could find that much, he'd do the dusting around the house a lot more often.

But the amazing part was, Miss Melba, gave each of the other ladies a third of the money she had found. She said she wouldn't have found it if they hadn't locked her in the restroom all night.

Wow. If Jan had found that much money, he sure wouldn't give it to his enemies. Although, he wasn't sure exactly what he would do with it. Steve would probably buy a used car with it.

What Miss Melba did was what Pastor Enoch at Jan's church would call showing Christian love and forgiveness. He always told their youth group that people didn't deserve to be saved from their sins, but God supplied forgiveness to those who'd believe. It was called grace --receiving what you didn't deserve. And since God was willing to show grace to us, we should be willing to show grace to our enemies too. It was hard for Jan to imagine.

Jan also had to read Dick Tracy, Dondi, and several of the funny comics too. At least, Jan could talk to Steve about reading those strips and the funny ones. Most boys and their dads read stuff like that. At least, that's what Jan had gathered from other guys' conversations when he sat near them at school a few years ago.

Of course, Sunday's comics were the best. They were bigger and in full color and had their own section. His dad had taught him the age-old tradition of how to read the Sunday comics properly.

Devout readers would lie down on the floor and spread the comics section out before them to enjoy. Sometimes, he and his dad had done this together. When they did, Jan could feel his dad's powerful shoulder muscles against his shoulder. They seemed to pass on strength to him even through their shirts.

Jan's mom arrived home a little after 5 p.m. from her job at AuSable Canoe Manufacturing.

Gunwale was called the canoeing capital of the world. At least, that's what advertisements said. Not only did it have a company which made them, but canoe liveries all over the town rented canoes to people in summer for trips down the river. Mostly downstate people, like from Detroit, did this to escape from the craziness of the big city. Many locals had their own canoes. Jan's dad's canoe was hanging from the rafters in the garage. It hadn't been used in years – not since the accident.

"Sue is going to the basketball game tonight with her friends. So, it is just you and me. I was thinking we'd just have pancakes for supper, Jan," said his mom as she puffed on her Virginia Slims cigarette. "Don't forget I have bowling."

"Yeah," came Jan's response. Pancakes would be good on his stomach also.

At suppertime, Jan came out of his bedroom, grabbed the newspaper from the couch, and placed it on his mom's tan chair in the living room. They sat down and ate quickly. His mom did most of the talking. The pink walls with white trim of the kitchen seemed to enhance her voice and presence.

Afterward, she walked into the living room and sat down briefly in her chair, fingering through the newspaper. She always had to read Dear Abby's column and then catch up with "Mary Worth" on the comics pages at the very least. She loved the lifestyles section also but didn't always have time for it. By 6:30, she was ready to leave.

"Now, you be good and get your schoolwork done," she said, studying the condition of her auburn hair in the mirror in the mudroom.

"I don't have any. It was the first day of our new semester today."

"Well, it wouldn't hurt to start reading through your new books. You tend to lose your focus on things a few weeks into the semester.

"Now, don't forget to lock the door when I leave." She tapped his shoulder with a hesitating motion.

It seemed as if she was afraid to touch him. As if he might be too fragile.

"Remember what your dad used to say, 'It's good to spend time by yourself. It makes you tougher.'" She turned and closed the door behind her.

His stomach felt heavy now. Once again, Jan was alone.

Except for the voice, of course. The negative voice wasn't always within hearing range, but it was there, hiding in the shadows, waiting for the right circumstances, or phrase spoken or feeling. Then, it would attack again.

Chapter 5

Jan trudged into the empty, dark living room with its lonesome furniture. His dad used to spend most of his time at home in this room, the small amount of time he was home, that is. Outside of the color TV set, the room's most outstanding feature was a large bookcase in the prominent corner.

Twenty-eight trophies filled most of the upper half of the case, except for one lonely, empty spot in the very center of the top shelf where dust collected. Some pictures of his dad smiling and holding trophies and a few of him running were on the lower shelves along with a scrapbook. On the very top lay a flag folded into three corners.

The large room had no ceiling light. It had to be lit by several table lamps and sometimes they failed to light the whole space well. The darkness Jan stood in sometimes reminded him of an old building in a western ghost town on movies he and his dad would occasionally watch together. The wounded cowboy hero would follow the trail of the villain into the abandoned community. Building by dark building he would search for the bad guy who could be behind any dark corner, waiting to kill him. With the gunshot wound in his leg or arm, the cowboy's chances of finding him felt so unlikely. Fear for the hero clung to Jan during those times. He could easily picture himself as the hero and Mark Fury as the villain.

Jan glanced around the room, concentrating in the dark corners and behind the furniture. At times, he thought he spotted something, but it seemed to vanish. He walked briskly out of the room and checked the locks on the doors again.

Suddenly, cobwebs in the corner of the kitchen ceiling blew upward as the furnace came on. That was Jan's signal. He walked into the kitchen and plopped down on the metal heat register on the floor beneath the clock to feel the warm air. He loved the heat from the furnace as it blew up into his shirt, warmed his belly and chest and then came out the top of his shirt blowing his orange hair, like a summer breeze. Jan loved the warmth. He knew that probably made him a sissy too. Guys were supposed to be tough and not feel cold or any other discomforts, but he just couldn't help how he felt.

Closing his eyes, he pictured himself walking through the trails next to the river again. The sun warmed his body and a light wind blew through his hair. Removing his shoes and socks, he waded through the cool water of the AuSable River. He could see fish swimming around his legs as if they were nothing more than fallen branches.

When he tired of wading, he would walk toward shore and sit down on one of the fallen trees along the river. There he would simply watch the river flow by. Birds hopped around; squirrels darted from tree to tree. Fish would leap up to snatch a bug floating on the water. And, on rare occasions, he might even see a beaver swim by, carrying branches in its mouth. Why couldn't life among people be that way? No one bothering anyone else. Everyone enjoying each other's company.

He opened his eyes and looked down. Warm air still blew up through his shirt. The scene of his bare chest underneath brought him back to reality. Not a single hair. Shame welled up inside again. He had gotten hair under his arms all right, but not a single hopeful one on his chest. His dad had had a bunch of them. He didn't know when they showed up though. Chest hair had to be a sign you weren't a sissy. No woman had those.

Jan glanced up at the kitchen clock. It wasn't even 7 p.m. yet. Steve was out with Jenny tonight. So, it would be a long evening at home for Jan. His favorite show, a science fiction program starring David McCallum, wouldn't be on for another hour. He had heard this would be the last episode. Seemed like the science-fiction shows were always the first to get canceled.

Standing back up, he walked back to his bedroom and gently sat down on his bed. His stomach still had that heavy, achy feeling, but the churning had stopped. The heavy school books on his desk stood like a gigantic tower before him. Start reading those tonight? Why? There would be enough school work for the rest of the semester.

He rolled over to his nightstand and opened the bottom drawer. Quickly, he grabbed the comic book at the top of the stack, "The Phantom" No. 3. He stared at the bright painted cover by artist George Wilson. The mighty hero held a shiny diamond cup.

His dad had once told him the Phantom's comic strip appeared in newspapers around the world. He had seen it in his travels with the army during World War II. In fact, The Phantom comic strip was smuggled into Norwegian newspapers while they were occupied by the Nazis. That kept the Norwegian people aware America was still alive and kicking while Nazis spread lies about our country's defeat. Dad also said there had been a Phantom movie serial during the 1940s. A Michigan movie actor named Tom Tyler played the part. Jan had always wanted to see it. During his 15 years, Jan saw only one cartoon where the Phantom appeared made an appearance. That was never enough for his favorite masked hero.

Jan's mom didn't care much for comic books. She felt they were too violent. However, she had made a concession with the Phantom. That was because both Jan and his dad had read the character's newspaper strip every day together.

Carefully, Jan flipped through the pages. The first story was about someone stealing the legendary diamond cup of Alexander and the Phantom getting it back. The second story, however, was about a boy who was bullied. The Phantom taught the boy how to protect himself and later the boy won a fight against the bully. Books, TV shows, and movies all showed the best way to handle a bully was to fight back.

But what about, "Turn the other cheek?" Jan wondered.

Jan knew it was better to show love than to strike out at someone, like Mark Fury. Somedays, though, it was as if fighting him seemed the only way to stop Mark from picking on him. Of course, if Jan lost, which he probably would (Mark had all those scars from fights he'd previously won), the bullying would continue anyway. So, what was the point?

And if he did turn the other cheek, but Mark kept hitting him, then what? Did God want Jan to do, just stand there? To just take it? God wanted men to turn the other cheek, but sometimes He wanted them to go to war too. So, what was a guy to do?

Jan just didn't like fights. He didn't want to hurt anyone. Fighting seemed pointless. Why did some of the other guys try to force him to? Of course, that was something else Jan was missing. The desire to fight. It was probably another sign of being a sissy. There were so many and he couldn't remember them all.

If he only had the Phantom's muscles, no one would pick on him. Bullies would take one look and back off. He had tried using some of his dad's old barbells once. After a week of it, he could hardly feel the difference though. So he gave up. Somedays, everything Jan did seemed pointless. Maybe barbells just didn't work on sissies. Maybe sissies were born with less muscle tissue.

* * * * * *

Teachers only gave a couple of homework assignments for the remainder of the week and Jan, trying to keep his promise to Mr. Guideron, finished, and turned them in on time. He was off to a good start so far. If only Mark Fury would leave him alone and his intestines wouldn't react, he would do okay. So far this day, his stomach just felt a little sensitive. That meant it was returning to normal.

Ever since he had come down with this disease, and his dad had left, his life seemed to follow a predictable pattern, at least in school. He would start out doing well, but as the semesters progressed he'd have more episodes of intestinal problems and everything became tougher. Sometimes, he thought about laying down in the road in front of his house, on the crest of a hill, and waiting for a car to come. That would end it.

Struggling came with this disease. He'd have some great days. Then on others, he'd spend most of his time in the bathroom, feeling weak. His strength seemed to go into the toilet along with his previous meals. He felt totally weak. Other days he felt hopeless, unable to do his work. On days others bullied him, he couldn't focus on work. All the symptoms took place on the inside where others could not see what was happening. He felt sure most teachers saw him as just lazy. An underachiever. Maybe sissies were underachievers too. He just couldn't figure out how to stop these cycles of illness.

Saturday morning finally came. Jan recharged himself with a bowl of cereal on the living room floor watching his three favorites Bugs Bunny, Scooby-Doo, and Shazam! on TV. He considered it a reward for surviving his first week of the new semester. Somehow those shows gave him hope.

Jan spent the early afternoon on Saturday hanging out with Steve over at his house. Basically, they sat on his twin beds and talked, while music played. Antique cars adorned the wallpaper in his room, along with dark blue drapes. There weren't many places to go in Gunwale in winter. They could go to Decker Drugs and buy sodas from the fountain, but as cold as it was outside a cold beverage didn't sound all that great. Living in a town of this size, they were used to not having many options though.

Being with Steve was another way of lightening up on the depression he felt on some days. Was it the power of friendship, as some syrupy movie might explain it? Jan couldn't be sure. All he knew was once they started talking and laughing, his depression would fade.

Steve and Jan had initially met the summer before first grade. In fact, they had almost literally ran into each other on their bikes as they

41

came up to a corner from different directions. Although they were the same age, there was almost an older brother-younger brother relationship between them. Yet their different skills and situations at home made them equal.

Steve was the oldest of two children, Jan the youngest of two. Neither had brothers. So, most of the time, Steve would teach Jan what he learned. Jan, on the other hand, was creativity incarnate. Together they made quite a team, imagination and know-how.

Both had parents who had grown up in the area. Steve's dad had started out as a real estate agent. He was doing well when some investment company came along and asked for his help in securing some property for a new industry. The company said they had big plans and encouraged Steve's dad, Mr. Reddy, and some other businessmen to invest in the new plant they intended to build.

In the end, the whole project turned out to be a scam. Mr. Reddy and the other men lost a lot of money. Most people in town had blamed Steve's dad for what went down, but, in fact, he had lost more money than anyone. That was when their family moved into Jan's neighborhood.

Mr. Reddy soon found a job as a used car salesman in town. But then, he started making trips to the Big Chief Hotel Lounge before coming home for supper. That's the way Jan had always thought of him since he knew him – coming home with difficulty walking and slurring his words.

The shadow of the scam hung over the Reddy family for several years. There were parents who wouldn't allow their children to play with Steve, for fear he might be untrustworthy, as they assumed his dad was. Jan could care less about the town's gossip however and his mom was just thankful for Jan just to finally have a good friend.

Once, when they were in fifth grade, they took their bikes and went exploring a wooded area across the river on another end of town. A dead-end road came off the Madsen Street and curved around some corners. A few scattered houses peaked out from trees along the left side of the road. On the right however, was just a big wooded area.

There were no Keep Out signs posted along the road. Just a big area of thick forest. Right at the dead-end, they found a trail going through the length of the woods, out to a well-used street.

Once inside they found a bunch of pine tree branches strewn around. It had been a harsh winter. Numerous pines had lost branches from an ice storm. Looking around at the results and a huge pine tree set back off the path suddenly gave Jan an idea.

They took the broken branches and leaned them against the huge pine. The simple structure became a natural teepee. It was, in fact, the perfect fort! The branches were tall enough, so they had plenty of headroom inside. It kept the rain out. The only sound they ever heard were squirrels and birds. They could hide their bikes behind the tree so no one could see them either. Even Steve's younger sister couldn't find them there.

Then came the fateful day everything fell apart. While sitting in their fort, they spotted an older man walking his hound and clearly surveying the area. His careful glances told them he was looking for something or someone specific. The boys looked at each other wide-eyed.

"Do you think this is his property?" Jan whispered.

"Kind of looked like it," said Steve.

As soon as he was out of sight and they could no longer hear him, they took off in the opposite direction where they had come from, pushing their bikes back up the hill. It was when they had almost made it to Madsen Street they heard some rustling bushes and the old man stepped out in front of them. Jan and Steve back-pedaled and brought their bikes to a stop. The old man let them know in no certain terms this was his property and trespassers weren't welcome. They nodded and bowing their heads left the area and the coolest fort ever behind.

When Jan became sick in seventh grade, it was Steve who stopped by to visit on a daily basis. Even when Jan was too sick to get out of bed, Steve would stop by to play a board game with him or just watch TV together. On better days, they would be out playing like usual. Fortunately, his doctor found the right medication for Jan, so he could live a halfway normal life again.

Jan and Steve didn't agree on everything of course. Steve stopped going to church in elementary school. His family used to attend the largest church in town, St. Thomas, with its gothic parapets and bright stained-glass windows. After the scam, the family was treated differently by parishioners there and finally left. No one in their house spoke about church or God now.

Two years ago, when they were thirteen, Steve called Jan over one day. He was especially cautious when he let Jan into his room. He and Steve could be quite sneaky when they wanted, but this seemed over-the-top for Steve. They sat down on the other side of Steve's bed, away from the door.

Steve reached under his bed and pulled out a stack of magazines. They were the nude kind – the ones that Decker Drugs always kept on the top shelf of their magazine display.

"My cousin snuck these over. He took them from his dad's garage. He says his dad's got lots more." Steve opened up one and began showing Jan pictures. Jan's eyes widened. He never thought he would ever see anything like that. Nothing was left out.

Yet, in spite of the sense of discovery came something else. He felt his face become warm. His breathing slowed. They weren't anything like any magazine photos Jan had seen before. Some were actually gross.

In the meantime, Steve had almost become a narrator for the photos. He seemed to know all about everything that was being shown. When had he become such an expert?

Then came the guilt. Jan felt like a peeping tom. He really didn't want to look anymore. But what should he say? Not wanting to look at the photos of women might raise some questions. The last thing Jan needed was to be tagged as one of those boys who didn't like girls.

Fortunately, there was a shout from the hallway. Steve's sister opened the door to announce supper was ready. Steve quickly scolded her for coming in without knocking. The magazines had returned to their hiding place without being seen. Jan breathed a sigh of relief and headed home for his own meal, feeling more than a little embarrassed. The rest of the night it was difficult to get those photos out of his head. From that point on, Jan kept some ideas in his head about what else they could do together, when in Steve's bedroom, to avoid the magazines.

Today, Jan and Steve just sat around on beds, listening to a new album Steve had bought. Steve loved his music, especially loud rock music. Jan preferred more calming music with a simple guitar or piano playing. When they spent time together, music choices never mattered. They talked of girls, of dreams, whatever popped into their heads at any given moment. Nothing else mattered.

When three o'clock came, Steve had to get ready to go see Jenny. Jan made his way home through the snow. His mom was off on some errands and said she'd be out having some dinner with her friends. Of course, Sue was always gone when Mom was. Frozen TV dinners packed the freezer for nights like this. With no worries, he sat down at his desk and took out some drawing paper. Tonight would be a fun night.

Chapter 6

On Sunday, Jan, Sue, and their mom attended church. Everyone sat quietly. Its sanctuary featured concrete block walls painted white, embellished by reddish colored wood trim. More reddish wood made up the ceiling, held in place with heavy wooden beams. While these walls resembled those at the high school, the soft white color combined with the wood taken from the forests surrounding their community gave off an atmosphere of peace. From the ruddy wood, rafters hung electric lights which could be dimmed or made brighter, depending on the mood of the service. On Good Friday, the lights were kept low for Tenebrae service, with a dark cloth hanging from the arms of the cross. Most of the time, lights brightened the whole area, making it possible to read hymnals and the Bibles in the pews.

Pastor Enoch rolled his wheelchair up onto the chancel. The congregation had redesigned the sanctuary when he came to be pastor a few years ago to make it easier for him to get around. Jan glanced around and spotted Barry Lancer and a few other teenagers from the youth group among the crowd. Pastor Enoch turned to face the congregation. He made a few announcements before starting the service. Most of it was about people who needed prayer. One item was about new library shelves.

"And, I don't want our youth to forget, we'll be going rollerskating at the rink down in Prudenville again on the second Sunday in February after church. So, bring your money for skate rental and pop. We'll provide the pizza."

The whole youth group was gripping their pew seats to keep from jumping up and down. Eyes were bright with excitement. Barry and Jan grinned at each other with smiles which barely covered their teeth.

In winter, the only activity which could top rollerskating was tubing. They had just been tubing during Christmas break. That special northern activity involved traveling down a snow-covered hill on a big inner tube. It was way faster than sledding and, unlike skiing, required no graceful form.

Pastor Enoch seemed to always know what the teenagers liked to do. And he played guitar, teaching teenagers modern Christian songs. He even played guitar during the worship service sometimes. Having Pastor Enoch was so different than previous pastors they had had who stuck with the King James Bible and ancient, slow-moving hymns.

He had a sense of humor too. His balding head, big oval glasses, and beard allowed him to make a wide range of funny faces as he talked. Unlike the comedians Jan had seen on TV, Rev. Enoch felt more down-to-earth, making life itself seem like a funny comic strip.

While previous pastors seemed untouchable, he would place his hands on people as he talked to them. He patted people on the back. During his sermons, he even spoke of his earlier life and what he called his "journey to knowing Jesus."

After the service, Jan gathered with Barry and some other teenagers in their corner of the big open room adults called the narthex. Barry and a couple of other guys talked about snowmobiling. Jan leaned back and listened, smiling as they got to the humorous parts.

In other areas of the large room, their parents were all talking with each other, divided up into groups of men and women. Then, Pastor Enoch came out and wheeled himself over to Jan's mother. He said something to her and she nodded her head. Suddenly, she turned to Jan and motioned for him to come over.

Curious, Jan plodded over to where his mom and the pastor were.

"Jan, Pastor has something he'd like to speak to you about."

Jan wondered if getting behind in homework was a sin. Maybe pastors gave warnings about such things?

"Jan, as you know, we're building some new library shelves. I can do a lot of the work, but I need help in reaching up to the higher spots. Would you mind stopping by after school on some days to help me out for a few weeks?"

Jan breathed a sigh of relief. "Sure." He knew nothing about building anything, but Pastor Enoch seemed plenty experienced at it. Jan could reach as well as anyone. They agreed to get together next Wednesday to make their plans for the new shelves.

Leaving the church, Jan's family made a quick stop to pick up the Sunday newspaper at Decker Drugs. Almost all the businesses downtown were closed Sundays. Decker's was one of the few opened because it had a soda fountain and sandwich bar. It also had the best selection of magazines, comic books and paperbacks in town. He paid Mr. Decker, a thin, sour-faced older man, with the change from his pocket. Mr. Decker seemed to have a soft spot for Jan because he always grabbed his Phantom comic books paid for them and left. Decker didn't like the kids who read the comics in his store but never bought them.

As he climbed back into the car, Jan's mom reminded him not to open the newspaper until they were inside the house. She didn't want to be picking up sections of newspaper all over the seats and floor of a cold car when they arrived. As soon as they were in the door, Jan ran to the sky blue, living room. Carefully, he peeled the colorful Sunday Comics Section from the front of the newspaper. The remaining sections were placed on the side table next to his mom's chair. Then, Jan bent down on his knees and placed the comics on the shag carpet in front of him. Excited, he lay down on his stomach to read. The art and bright colors drew him in.

Detective Dick Tracy, famous for wearing his signature yellow trench coat and fedora, was on the trail of a new gang of thieves. This one happened to be an all-female gang. They shot ink into the banks' security cameras, so they could not be identified. The latest eyewitness to one of their robberies had been abducted in his hospital room while he was being interviewed by Tracy's son, Junior, a police sketch artist. This all-female gang had gotten into the hospital by disguising themselves as nurses.

In the bottom half of the strip, the scene switched the gang's hideout. Inside, their leader Lispy was leading the girls in a cheer. The cheer talked about how they were smarter, tougher and braver than men. Then, a mouse ran by and they shrieked. Lispy blasted it with her shotgun. Jan's dad would have roared with laughter reading that. He thought the whole idea of women using guns was preposterous. To his dad's mind, women were too fragile to use guns.

Jan quickly moved on to other comics strips like the Phantom and Dondi, and funny ones too like Peanuts, Blondie, and Hagar the Horrible. As he finished up, he sat up and leaned over to set the comics section down on the coffee table in front of the couch where Sue rested. Her hand quickly shot out and tore them from Jan's, before the paper even had a chance to touch the wood surface.

Jan leaned back and stared up at the ceiling. He had an idea of what would follow. Sue suddenly huffed.

"What a chauvinist!" she exclaimed. "This cartoonist for Dick Tracy is putting women down. Showing them as weak and scared. I don't believe this!"

"Oh, Sue. It's only a comic. If you don't like it, read something different. There's plenty in there."

"You don't understand, Mom. This is sexist propaganda. We talked about it in Ms. Appenij's sociology class. This is as bad as what the Nazis did in World War II."

"Oh, please, Sue."

"It's true. You know, there are some people who believe the Bible is just propaganda written by men to keep women from reaching their full potential."

"It's a pretty big book for a purpose so little as that, Sue."

Jan relaxed and smiled. He was staying out of that conversation.

Today's Dick Tracy strip did make women with guns look like a silly idea. However, Tracy had battled a number of male villains who weren't so bright either. Jan could not help but laugh a little at Sue because she always acted so tough until she needed him to help to kill spiders in her room. He would hate to see her with a gun.

Still, there were a couple of tomboys in Jan's neighborhood who were pretty tough and good at sports. If he were in a war, he would want them on his side. What a picture that would make. Jan with a gun in a war. He couldn't even bring himself to go hunting. So, did that make the tomboys more manly than he was? It seemed like there were a lot of people – even girls – who would say yes.

* * * * * *

A bitter cold weather system hung over Gunwale as the next week began. Wednesday morning was no exception. Even without the blizzard-like winds of the first day of the semester, the chill in the air itself turned Jan's ears blood red and seemed to draw water from his eyes. His nose had no feeling left by the time he and Steve reached the middle school to await their bus. He wished he could be back on the heat register in the kitchen again.

Jenny gave Steve a big hug when she arrived. When they kissed, Jan could tell they were using their tongues. He turned away until they finished. Really guys? In front of everybody?

Steve had started dating early. It was in upper elementary school sometime. Anyhow, the guy had no fear at all. If one girl turned him down for a date, he'd simply ask another. On the same day. Whenever his family took summer vacations with their camping trailer, Steve would meet some new girl who he'd take down some forest trail to teach her about nature.

Then, he met Jenny as a freshman and they became a couple. It looked as if Steve's Don Juan days were finally over, but it was more like just a hiatus. When Jenny was unavailable, Steve returned to his old ways, usually with visiting girls from out of town.

Sometimes Jan felt sorry for Jenny. So much went on behind her back. Yet, whenever Steve was with her, it was as if she were the only girl in the world for him. How could he do that?

All Jan knew is he would never treat a girl that way. If there ever would be one who liked him. Maybe, in the whole world, there might be one. Whatever Steve had to attract all those girls Jan certainly did not possess.

Modern U.S. History went as well as usual. More lecturing by Mr. Gray. Jan's second-hour class was Biology. It was his second-most-hated class. He didn't know how he would get around dissecting animals.

Jan's dad had taken him rabbit hunting a few times. Try as he could, Jan simply could not pull the trigger on the rabbits running by. Even more, proof he had become what his father never wanted. Still, Jan went with him, just to be alone with his dad. They would cruise down old trail roads and his dad would tell him stories about the area. He missed those little adventures.

Then third hour arrived. It was the part of the school day Jan dreaded. Gym class students stood in line in their cutoff jeans and t-shirts, mostly facing the coach, as he called out their names. Some of the guys were joking and punching each other. Others were like racehorses just waiting for their gate to open. Barry Lancer stood with a guy on each side of him talking. There was no way for Jan to squeeze in around them without looking awkward. Mark Fury was there too, joking around with another guy, fortunately.

It was scary waiting to find out what embarrassing activity was on Coach's agenda for the day. Jan's hands were cold and clammy. Even with the other guys talking around him, what he mostly heard, or maybe felt, was his heartbeat and breathing. He wanted to run away to some unseen corner and just watch.

He hated being in large groups of guys like this. Jan felt like David against a whole army of Goliaths, who had just not noticed him yet. It would not matter how many stones he had. He doubted he could even figure out how to use a slingshot anyway. His mom felt they were too dangerous.

Jan looked around at the guys surrounding him. Well-defined muscles stood out from their arms and legs as declarations of their manliness. What if one of these guys suddenly just turned and started belting Jan for the fun of it? What would stop them? Would Coach do anything? Or would he just laugh with the other guys he coached? Sometimes, he seemed like just a bigger version of them. Like one of their pals.

Just give us something to do independently, Coach, he pleaded inside his head. This was supposed to be Boys Individual Sports after all. And his last gym requirement. So far, he had managed to survive the previous classes with minimal embarrassment.

"All right!" shouted Coach in his low voice. "Today, I'm going to be writing down bench press stats for everyone. You should be able to bench press your own body weight. For those who are unable to yet, you'll be required to work toward that goal this semester. For those who can already bench press their body weight, you will be required to increase your current level by 25 percent.

"First, I want everyone to move down to the scales by the locker room door. I'm going to record each of your weights and then we'll head upstairs to the weight room where we'll record what your current weight lifting ability is."

The football players and wrestlers roared like a crowd of spectators. Some began challenging the guys next to them to competitions and placing five-dollar bets.

No! No! Do we have to do this as a group? Couldn't he just take a few people, or even better, one person at a time to do this. Everybody else could shoot baskets or something. Why did there have to be such a big audience for this?

Again he wanted to run off, but he could not. Instead, he wiped his wet palms against the legs of his cutoffs.

Jan kept looking at the clocks while the coach recorded weights. He wished he had telekinesis like some people he had read about. Then he would move the arms of the clock forward about 20 minutes or so, just enough time for the class to end too early for him to be called up.

Everyone soon marched upstairs. The weight room was just a caged-in area, like an enclosure at a zoo. Everyone gathered around the single weight machine to watch. Jan kept himself behind the large group, leaning against the cement-block wall. Maybe the coach would miss his name on the list. It had happened before.

Then the calling began as each guy stepped forward to prove who he was as a man. Jan felt the cold painted cement blocks in the wall behind him. The indentations felt like scars. How did blocks get scars?

"A hundred and five!" called the coach's assistant as little Joey Montmorris sat up. His job stacking shelves at the A&P grocery store must have some benefits, Jan thought.

Guys muttered their approval, some even amazement, at the weight the skinny kid had mastered.

Calls kept coming in as each guy took his turn.

"One twenty-five!"

"One fifty!' As the numbers went up, the volume of other guys' voices increased.

"Two-thirty!" came the shout from the assistant as Burke Johnson stood up. Several guys cheered. Some clapped. Burke strutted off, messing up some other guy's hair.

"Jan Richards," called the coach.

Jan laid down on the warm bench. The foam rubber within inside brought little comfort. He could feel the eyes of his audience upon him. He could almost hear their internal voices shouting, "Prove yourself! Prove yourself!"

His sweaty palms gripped the handlebars of the bench press above his shoulders. Why bother with this? He already knew what the results would be. A big F. Failure. Once again, he would prove to the world he was only pretending to be a guy. He didn't belong with the rest of them. He couldn't earn his place.

Jan pushed upward with all his might, but it was like trying to push against the concrete wall. Nothing.

The coach's assistant, Tim, took the key out and raised it to the next lighter weight.

Again he tried. Again complete failure.

As other guys shifted on their feet and breathed impatient sighs, Tim the assistant kept moving the key, farther and farther up the weight load. Yet, he hardly felt a difference the higher up the key went.

85, no. 75, no. 60, no.

Oh, just mark me with an F! Get it over with. Why? Why did they make kids do this? He asked himself.

It was bad enough knowing he wasn't much of a man. Why did he have to prove it in front of so many others. In other classes, he could at least pretend. But, here, his disguise was ripped off by the strong hands of truth. The truth was cruel.

He pushed again, his teeth showing, his forehead tightening into ripples of frustration. Then, it gave. The weights went up. At last. Jan breathed out and slowly set the weights down again.

"Fifty-five," he heard the assistant say.

"Fifty-five," repeated the coach.

Fifty-five out of a hundred thought Jan. Yeah. Another failure.

"Someone needs to send him some condolences flowers," came a whisper among them.

Mark Fury chuckled.

"Quiet," said Coach.

Jan couldn't make eye contact eye contact with anyone at that point. There was total silence.

Like at a funeral.

Warm shame rose from his feet, made its way up to his legs, tossed his stomach, and drowned his heart. It settled in his throat making him feel like he might drown. His breathing became shallow.

Jan went and stood behind the crowd of onlookers and against the cold cement wall for the rest of the hour. There was nothing quite like hiding behind the enemy for safety. Finally, the class came to an end.

Locker rooms always smelled like disinfectant and felt cold. The cement walls and floor, the metal lockers and even the wood benches gave the feel of being locked in a refrigerator. Worst yet was the fact that they made you take a shower in a large, open room where everyone could learn all about you. And it made for a cold stage. Jan never did well in any type of comparison with other guys. Not weight-lifting, not in basketball, not in football. Nothing. Mark Fury was right.

After most of the other boys had started dressing to leave and Mark had already taken off, Jan took off his gym clothes. He walked forward into the cold room with the wet floor, where water had flowed off of other boys' bodies. His eyes kept focused straight on the nearest shower head. Once he stood in front of the wall it would be harder for anyone to see him and his laughable excuse for a male physique.

Jan looked down at his body. Back in seventh-grade, when boys first had to take showers, he was shocked by how different guys' bodies were. His friend Steve looked like a man by the time he was 14. Mark Fury wasn't far behind. Jan kept thinking he looked more like an 11-year-old at the time.

Mark Fury was right. Jan's body still looked way too small and fragile even now. Jan just wasn't sure if it was his fault or a punishment from God.

Outside, by the lockers, he heard the other guys laugh. It was probably about him.

Chapter 7

When Jan stepped off the bus at the middle school after the ride back into town, he questioned whether he should go to the church to help Pastor Enoch or not. Nothing in him wanted to be around people. He could feel a dark shadow over his soul. His soul was crouching in its hiding place again when the negative voice in his head spoke up again.

What about when Pastor Enoch finds out you know nothing about building stuff? What will he think of you? Obviously, that isn't normal for a boy. Every other guy can at least build minor things, like birdhouses. You barely passed shop class. Sissy.

Jan knew he could just go home and call Pastor. He could say he wasn't feeling well. Then, what? A lonely house? He didn't even feel like reading comics.

The church was only two blocks away. His house was more like four and across the busy Bateau Avenue. He might meet Mark on the way too. Steve was a ways down the block in another direction, walking Jenny home. Jan really did not want to disappoint Pastor.

Finally, he moved his feet forward. Pastor Enoch always made him feel warm and cared for. Maybe it would be better to follow the plan they had made. Still, there was a tingling feeling in Jan's arms and his brain felt like it was giving off warning signals as he walked along.

On the right side of the first block sat a group of family homes set closely together, almost like a row of lockers. To his left stood a pair of imposing homes built by the lumber barons who made their money cutting down the great pines before Gunwale was established.

The second block ahead on the left featured the local Catholic church, spreading out its wings and taking up the whole block. Across the street stood a single house, a large parking lot and then Jan's church at the very end. The small structure, only a fraction of the size of its Catholic neighbor, stood proudly.

Jan's church was a white, concrete structure with wood embellishments for trim. The structure had an L shape with the longer part running against the back of the lot and the shorter section coming out to greet the sidewalk.

As he walked along Jan tried to just study the houses and other structures. If he let his mind go, that negative voice would return, reminding him of all his shortcomings as a guy. He had been a prisoner of that most of the day already.

Soon, he pulled open the wooden door to the church which led into a brief, wood-paneled hallway and past the pastor's office and the restrooms. Straight ahead stood the narthex, a big open area where people gathered after the service and they sometimes held potlucks. Its outer wall featured painted cement block with wood trim, similar to the outside. The other walls featured the same paneled wood near the Pastor's office. At the far end, a small kitchenette with a serving bar welcomed people. In the far right corner stood a simple bookcase stuffed with books. That was what Pastor wanted to replace. His plan was to build a series of bookcases in the opposite corner, where there was more wall space. That area of the room had been cleared out already.

"Hello, Jan," said the pastor from his wheelchair at a folding table in the center of the room.

"Hi."

"I thought today we would just plan out our shelves. So, we'll start by taking some measurements and figuring out how much shelf space we will need."

Jan smiled. Measuring? That was all? Jan breathed out and relaxed his shoulders. The tingling in his arms appeared to be lightening too. He could do that.

"Your dad wasn't much of a carpenter, was he? I don't remember him ever talking about it."

"No. He spent a lot of time at his jobs."

"That's okay. The first thing I need you to do is go down into the basement and measure the total amount of space the surplus books we have down there take up. I've already figured out the amount of space needed for the books we have up here in that corner. We want to create enough space up here for those and future books as well."

He handed Jan a tape measure, a small piece of paper and a stubby pencil. Jan quickly turned and tromped the basement steps located to the side of the sanctuary. At the bottom was a big central area surrounded by Sunday school classrooms. On the nearest wall to the steps stood a lone bookcase, filled with books, and then piles of books around it.

Jan set the pencil and paper on the floor and pulled out the measuring tape to begin his work. He measured the first shelf and wrote down the figures on the paper. Then he measured the second. Same measurements. Oh, yeah, he realized, that makes sense.

Smiling with pride, Jan multiplied the number of shelves by the size of the first shelf of books. Simple! Then he began to measure the piles of books around it, recording each one separately. Within just a few minutes, he was finished with the measurements.

As he looked at his figures on the paper, he realized he had done everything in inches. Was carpentry supposed to work that way? Or was Pastor expecting him to already have converted the information to feet by the time he went upstairs? Or did he need them in inches to calculate the size of the shelves? Jan hesitated on the first step. He didn't want to look stupid.

"How is it going, Jan?" came the pastor's gentle voice.

"Um. I haven't finished all the math yet."

"That's okay. Just bring it up here and let's take a gander at it."

Again, Jan breathed out. He tromped up the steps and entered the narthex. The pastor was sitting at the small table smiling at him with some blank typing paper spread out on the table.

"Let's see what ya got there."

Pastor Enoch studied Jan's calculations.

"Great job, Jan."

Jan smiled even bigger.

Pastor slid a calculator over to Jan. "Let's see how much shelf space we need."

Jan pressed the buttons as Pastor read the figures. Tapping "total," Jan slid the calculator back over to the cleric.

"Great balls of fire, Jan! That's more than I thought. We'll definitely need four units for all these books."

Jan smiled a big smile, almost laughing at the exaggerated way Pastor said that.

Soon he was planning out the shelving unit with Jan. Pastor explained what types of wood pieces were needed to make the units stable and attach them to the wall. It actually didn't look too difficult to Jan. Maybe he could be of help after all.

"Well, I suppose, if Noah had enough faith to build a whole ark with just three sons, you and I should have enough faith to build four bookshelf units."

"I guess so."

"You guess so?!" said the pastor with mock indignation. "Have faith, Jan! God can do anything with anyone. Even me!" He crossed his eyes and made a goofy smile which his grizzly beard exaggerated. Jan laughed.

"I don't think I would have made it as Noah, to be honest. He just did what God said. I'd be more like Gideon." Pastor paused for a moment. "Have you ever read about the life of Gideon, Jan?"

Jan shook his head.

"You've got to do that sometime. Judges 6 and 7. One of my

favorite reminder stories. Gideon thought he was the weakest man in all the land and there was no way God could use him. He's was just hopeless."

"Really?"

"Oh, yeah. It's funny though. People get this idea that in the Bible God called great people. Truth is they weren't any different than you or I. In fact, often they were messed up people. Gideon was in hiding from his enemies when God came to him. He had a difficult time trusting God too. But God has this way of taking the most unlikely people and using them in powerful ways."

God using scared people – sissies? Jan didn't remember hearing about that before. He remembered sermons God commanded men to be brave. But telling a sissy to be brave? Sissies were cowards. Where in the world did they find any courage? Jan never felt like he had any. Perhaps there was more to the stories in the Bible than Jan knew.

Suddenly, a thought came to him. "Pastor …."

"Yes, Jan?"

"Have you heard some people say that the Bible is something men made up to keep women under their control?"

"Oh, yes. That's a popular myth these days. Some people take the words of the Bible out of context."

"What do you mean by context?"

"Let me give you an example. There are places in the New Testament where it says women should remain quiet during the service. Some men have used verses like this to keep power over women and to keep them from participating in worship services. It's been going on for centuries.

"However, it is important to know the reason behind this verse. If we look back at the whole passage, we learn there were some women who would disrupt the services with their talking. Obviously, it happened a lot. So, Paul is correcting these women. Remember, many books of the New Testament were written as letters to address specific issues within the church."

Jan nodded.

"There will always be some people who will alter the meaning of the Bible or any law, for their own selfish reasons. That doesn't mean the law is wrong. The problem is those people are wolves in sheep's clothing. They are abusers who take advantage of women. That is why it is very important for us to understand what the Bible is actually saying by reading it to understand it."

"Oh," Jan pondered those words. "Do you think that's why this whole women's liberation movement got started? Because of abuse?"

The pastor stretched out his arm and clasped Jan's shoulder. "That's very perceptive of you, Jan. Yes. Many of the women I have counseled over the years who are into this movement were abused by men, sometimes several men. And not just boyfriends or husbands, but fathers, brothers, other family members, friends of the family. Then these women were betrayed by their own family who refused to believe the abuse was going and did nothing to help them. I think this movement was originally set up on the backs of bruised and battered souls."

"I don't like some of the things they say about men though."

"Neither do I. Some of them are very cruel, debasing all men. They forget men can be wounded too. You see, revolutions also wound the innocent. And wounded people often strike out in anger.

"For centuries even before our time, too many men have gone to church on Sunday but during the week drank excessively, brawled, abused their wives, lusted after other women, cussed, treated their neighbors cruelly showed no mercy. All of that is denounced by God in His Word. These men thought going to church once a week made them good Christians. Yet their lives showed no evidence of wanting to follow God. They just followed their own desires. They walk down a path to their own destruction, not to heaven.

"That is why I keep telling people to read the Bible for themselves. A trip to hear a sermon once a week won't change anyone. Only spending time in the Scriptures really changes people."

"Sometimes, I don't understand the Bible, though."

"Keep in mind, Jan, reading the Bible is not like reading a novel or self-help book. We need to seek God when we read it. Look for His message. Surrender ourselves to it by doing what He says."

"What do you mean by surrender?"

"Jesus said to pick up our cross daily and follow Him. We must put aside our own thoughts and ideas and search for Him in His Word. Follow what He says.

"If we want a world with more love and compassion, but also justice for wounded souls – whether they are women or men – we need to seek God with all our heart."

The words made a calmness fall upon Jan. It was like a hug to his soul. Pastor Enoch's teaching actually made sense. There was a hopefulness to it.

Before they knew it, the clock showed the time approaching five o'clock. Saying good-bye, Jan scooped up his school books and pushed open the outside door. The sky had gone from a white color to more of a gray, as the sun dropped lower. By 5 o'clock, it would be dark. Another part of winter he hated. The sun would come up just as he was leaving for school and it would set only about an hour and a half after they arrived home.

He missed the long hours when he would be on the trails along the river. He loved to run up and down those trails and explore the forested area between the trails and the river. He was just more cautious these days in avoiding kids like Mark Fury. It had been quite a while since he had seen him down there.

During winter, Jan missed the trails along the river. Sometimes it felt like another world, with mostly white and red pines and cedars. Some places in the wooded areas between the trail and the river were even dark from trees blocking out the sun. There were times he would sit down behind some fallen trees and just watch the river, animals, and even people who walked down the trail. The trees hid him perfectly. Although the animals might sense him, kids walking by never knew he was there. When he was younger, he would pretend he was Dick Tracy watching for a criminal.

All the snow Gunwale received in the winter filled in the trails though. There was no way to get through. It would be April at least before he could even attempt to run down the trails again.

He tromped down Spruce Street, still grinning to himself. The middle school was directly ahead. At least he could see the gym. Once he reached it, he'd turn left, go down about a block and turn right to aim himself toward home.

Then, he spotted a couple of kids hanging out on the school steps as he rounded the corner to go left. Quickly, he dropped his head low and stared at the snow-covered sidewalk. The attempt failed.

"Hey, Richards!"

The voice belonged to "Weasel" Birler. He was a short kid from Jan's grade who Jan always thought looked like Bluto (from "Popeye" cartoons). Weasel had the same coal, black hair and heavy eyebrows. He was also the first guy in Jan's class to grow facial hair. When he smiled, he looked like a mini Bluto.

Weasel's real name was Vince. He was known for getting into trouble at school and in the community in general. Jan also had a history of trouble with Weasel, going back to elementary school. One time, Jan was walking home. Weasel came up behind him with another kid, who Jan didn't know, and grabbed his packet of school pictures. As they struggled, the paper envelope ripped. Photos went everywhere. Jan retrieved most, but Weasel and his pal ran off with one sheet of photos.

A couple of blocks later he saw the boys in someone's backyard between some bushes. After seeing Jan, they ran off giggling but did not seem to have the sheet anymore. Making sure they had left the spot for good, Jan walked over to where they had been standing. On the grass was the sheet of photos all wet, with some drops of yellow liquid running down it. He left them on the ground and moved on.

Jan kept walking past the school now, staring at the road. Maybe if he ignored him, Weasel would lose interest. That is when he felt the whack against his back. Tiny pieces of ice-cold snow sprang up and dropped down between his neck and coat collar. Several more snowballs struck his back, but with his winter coat he hardly felt them.

Just as he figured he was out of their range, however, he felt something hard and cold strike behind his ear. He stumbled forward, losing his balance on some ice. Hitting the road in front of him, he tried to catch his breath. Then, came the sound of footsteps behind him. He felt some pain as a boy's knee pinned down his calf. A hand grabbed him by the hair and jerked his head up. Before he knew what was happening, a second hand appeared with a snowball in it.

Weasel took the wad of snow and jammed it into Jan's face. Some went into his mouth. The rest felt like an ice-cold scrub cloth against his face. The ice pellets rubbed his cheeks raw as he struggled to get away. The full weight of the boy on his calf made that impossible.

"Hey! Lay off him!" came a shout from a short distance away.

Immediately, Weasel released Jan. He and his pal took off running. Jan saw one of the male teachers from the middle school dashing toward him. Quickly, he grabbed his school books and ran off too, spitting ice crystals from his mouth. Fighting meant suspension from school. It didn't matter who started it.

Jan put as much energy into his legs as he could find. Soon the teacher's footsteps were gone. He had managed to get away. Stopping momentarily behind a tree, Jan took out his inhaler and forced a couple of puffs into his mouth. The teacher appeared to have left the street. Jan walked down a couple blocks, taking the long way home.

At least he had avoided getting taken to the principal's office. He could remember his previous encounters with Principal Evans when he was in middle school. They had happened in mid-semester both times, when his grades were low. The principal just kept telling Jan how lazy he was, how he was hiding behind a fake illness and how ashamed his parents must be of his grades. Of course, at that point, there was only his mom.

Jan rounded the corner over by the elementary school and ran down the hill toward home. Once inside, he quickly kicked off his shoes, ran back to his bedroom, and leaped onto the bed. Again, his hands reached out and gripped the edges of the bed. He pressed his raw cheek gently against the soft pillow.

Afraid We Are Not

Chapter 8

It was great when Sunday finally arrived. Jan, Sue, and his mom went to church early. Pastor Enoch spoke on Psalm 44:15 for his sermon that day, "My dishonor is continually before me, And the shame of my face has covered me." The whole congregation seemed to love what he had to say about shame and God.

Right after church, Pastor, few parents, and the youth group hopped into a few cars. (Sue decided to go home.) In a flash they took off 30 miles down the road to Prudenville for rollerskating. If rollerskating had been considered a sport, then Jan could actually say he liked one sport. No competition. They just rolled around the roller rink to the sound of music. Simple.

The owner of the rink, a middle-aged man with crew-cut hair, wore roller skates himself and sometimes joined others out on the rink floor while his wife handled customers and changed the music. When not on the floor, he made announcements from a booth at the front. Sometimes, he called for a couples skate, or a reverse skate or something else to change things around.

Sometimes, the owner's daughter was there. She wore this ice-skating outfit like Jan had seen when there were ice-skating competitions on TV. Her skills seemed to be on almost the same level as theirs. The pizza was great. Everyone sat down together and ate. It didn't matter where he sat. Jan looked around at everyone. The youth group was small but friendly. No bullies. No cliques. Just teenagers who shared the same faith and saw each other as good people. If only school could be more like that. It was one of those afternoons Jan wished would never end.

And, why not? They could just have school here. Pastor could be their teacher. The only students in his classes would be those around him. Gym would just be rollerskating. If only.

* * * * * *

On Wednesday, after school, Jan ran to the church as soon as he leaped off the bus. Inside the narthex, everything had been all cleared out except for one table, which Pastor Enoch sat at. A tarp was spread across a portion of the floor. On top of that was a couple of sawhorses and an electric saw. Beside those, on the tarp, was a stack of eight-inch boards ready for use.

"You're here early, aren't you?" the pastor asked.

"Well, I kind of ran."

The pastor chuckled. "I'm glad you're excited about this. I am too."

Pastor Enoch had Jan pick up some boards. They checked the measurements they had made on paper from the previous week and measured the boards. Jan marked where they needed to be cut using a metal square.

"So, has your body recovered yet from Sunday?"

"Yeah. I'm doing good. I think everyone had a good time rollerskating."

Jan paused briefly and then added, "Everyone really liked your sermon too. When I got home that night my mom was still talking about it."

"Shame is something we can all identify with. We all have it.

67

Although I'm not sure Sue's sociology teacher, Ms. Appenij, would have appreciated my sermon as much as my congregation did."

"No?"

"Modern psychology would have us think shame comes just from experiences we've had in life and most often from the way, our parents raised us. I can't totally agree with that view."

"Why?"

"Well, the first mention of shame in the Bible is after Adam and Eve sin. Most people tend to think the shame the couple felt is only associated with their nakedness, but I think it goes farther than that and deeper than that, Jan. I believe shame is part of sin. It is part of who we are now. Shame is God's way of reminding us that we are not all who we were meant to be. It shows us somewhere deep inside we are lacking in something."

"But doesn't the Bible say they were ashamed of being naked?"

"Absolutely, Jan. But you see, we humans tend to focus the blame on something more tangible. Like other people, circumstances, and even our bodies. The realization that they were naked was just a symptom of how their lives had been changed by sin. Sin was part of them at that point. That shame they felt was a reflection of how they had changed."

"So, sometimes we can blame our bodies for what we don't understand?"

"Our bodies can become symbols for something else we are ashamed of."

"But, what about if someone says something about someone else's body. Can't that make them feel ashamed of themselves too?"

"Oh, yes. While shame is part of our sinful nature, it is added to by others throughout our lives. People can be cruel. I'm sure you know that."

"It's sad some people have to be like that."

"Most of us are that way, but we don't admit it to ourselves. We waver between abuser and victim. Shame is part of who we all are. We don't like it. Our frustration in not being able to deal with our shame leads to anger with ourselves."

"Huh."

"Like Adam and Eve, people today want to find someone else to blame for their hurts. They feel unable to overcome that feeling of shame. Unfortunately, they strike out at others in their frustration, hurting the innocent as well. However, hurting another person just increases their shame and causes them to feel even angrier. So, we perpetuate this on-going cycle of shame and anger in each other."

"Why don't people just stop doing that?"

"They are caught in a cycle."

"Can anything stop the cycle?"

"First, we must realize what caused the cycle in the first place. Sin. That's where shame came from. So, that is where we must start."

"Looking at our sin?"

"Right! And what did we say our sin reminded us of in our Bible study a couple of weeks ago?"

"That we need a Savior."

"Why is that, Jan?" Pastor asked.

"Because we are dead in our sins. A dead person can do nothing on his own. Someone else must do everything for him," said Jan grasping the recent memory.

"Exactly. So, you have been listening at youth group meetings. Sometimes, with you teenagers, I am not sure."

Jan grinned and breathed a brief laugh.

As soon as he reached home, Jan grabbed the newspaper from its plastic box on a metal pole near the end of the driveway and darted inside across the snow-covered pathway. On the comics page, the Phantom was hot on the trail of the men who had stolen the huge Star of Bangalla diamond. Three men were taking it to a nearby foreign prince to get money out of it. The Witchman had eliminated his partners along the way and planned to keep all the money from the diamond for himself. The Phantom was now heading for the palace in a jungle canoe.

Meanwhile "Dick Tracy" had gotten very exciting in the past few days. Lispy's all-female gang had made another robbery. This time, Detective Tracy and his partner Sam Catchem were only a few blocks away when it happened. There was a chase scene. Tracy leaped on to a passing lumber truck to get a better view of the gang's vehicle ahead of them. With a single shot, he caused the gang's car to veer off the highway. Just then, a low overpass came into view from the lumber truck. Tracy ducked and grabbed a chain to hold on. He barely escaped being decapitated.

Brenda Starr and her husband Basil decided to leave their room finally to dine at the Captain's table on ship. Meanwhile, the ship's crew was finding items missing. Some pillows, some blankets, and food were unaccounted for. It looked like there might be stowaways onboard.

Dondi, the war orphan boy, and his grandparents were being held captive by the villainous Mr. Hudson and his rebel soldiers. Hudson was after some hidden pirate treasure and he was forcing poor Dondi to help him find it. It kind of reminded Jan of the book, "Treasure Island."

Life felt hopeful again.

Chapter 9

The weather grew bitter cold again in Gunwale the next week. Temperatures were below zero. Local news broadcasts were sharing record lows in many surrounding towns. And Jan's mom's car wouldn't start that morning. Fortunately, she caught a ride with one of her co-workers.

With the continual blizzards and lake effect snow, snowbanks along the roads and driveways were up to at least three feet tall now. If the snowfall kept going as it was, it would soon be difficult to see down the street when backing out of the drive. Jan's mom and older people hated that point of winter.

The snowmobilers, however, loved it. They would take whatever snow they could get. The longer winter lasted the better, as far as they were concerned.

Jan was just about to take off for Steve's house when he caught a glimpse of Mark Fury coming down the street in his dark winter coat. Mark's feet stomped with ferocity and his arms swung rigidly. A frown covered his forehead, pressing his eyes into little slots. Jan could almost picture a tornado above Mark's head with lightning flashing around it and trees cowering in fear.

Jan waited for him to pass and get a good block ahead before coming out of the door. What could have gotten him upset so early? Somehow today, Jan needed to be on the lookout.

As he stepped out into the snowy street, the smell of wood-burning furnaces lingered in the air all around him. Jan heard a train bellow as it came into town several blocks away, over near the courthouse at the end of Bateau Avenue. The sky was blue and the sun shining down upon the little town. The cold made the experience far less enjoyable, however. In Northern Michigan, sunshine only meant warmth in summer. Sunshiny days in winter usually meant bitter cold. It seemed like the warmest days in winter were cloudy and depressing.

Still, Jan felt pretty positive today. The shelf construction with Pastor Enoch was going great. Steve's secret girlfriend from downstate, Mindy, came up but didn't bring a friend with her. So, Jan didn't need an excuse to turn down a double date.

Maybe this friend was a nice girl, but it would be difficult to be forced into a date with someone you didn't know. According to Steve's verbal journal, he and Mindy mostly made out and they sounded like they were coming very close to actually having sex.

Jan hadn't even kissed a girl. Or even held hands. He could not even begin to imagine becoming physical with one. He would rather get to know a girl first and then ask her out because they liked each other. Besides, Pastor Enoch and the Bible had always said sex was just for marriage. There must be a reason for that.

Jan and Steve were virtually out the door of Steve's house as soon as Jan arrived.

"I gotta show you something," said Steve as soon as they were in the street. He took out a piece of newspaper page he had ripped. It was from the classifieds section of the local newspaper and one item was circled.

"Look at this, Jan! A blue '69 Ford Maverick for sale. Only $600. I almost have that saved up now!"

"But you don't get your driver's license for a few months. Even if you bought it now, you couldn't drive it."

"Yeah, but I'd have it! I could hop in it as soon as I got my license and take off!"

Jan smiled at Steve's enthusiasm. He had no problem picturing Steve zipping down the street in a car. And he'd be right beside him -- like those cool cops on TV. They'd be out stump-jumping, exploring every trail road in the county. About seventy percent of the land in Gunwale County was state-owner forest land. That meant there was plenty to explore.

He and Steve looked at each other with goofy grins. The grins just spread out farther as they saw each other's faces. Yep, exploring every two-track in the county.

As usual, Jenny joined them at the middle school. Jan could see Mark Fury at the end of the line talking to other guys. As long as Jan stayed with Steve and Jenny, there shouldn't be any problems. They had only talked for a few minutes when the bus pulled up to the line. A herd of middle schoolers trampled off in quick fashion. The high schoolers then began to hop on. As Jan stepped forward, his books slipped through between his arm and side. He stopped to pick them up, causing a bunch of other students to get on before him.

When he finally jumped on board, he noticed the seats around Steve and Jenny had all been taken.

Breathing a sigh, he made his way toward the back. There were still lots of empty seats yet. One person stood, bent over, in the far back sorting through some books and papers with their back turned to everyone else.

So, Jan plopped down onto a cold vinyl seat. He set his books down beside him. All his homework had been finished except for one assignment. He planned to finish that in study hall. The day was starting off well.

"Everybody in their seats," called the bus driver. "We can't leave until everyone is sitting down."

Jan heard the person behind him scuffle their shoes for a moment, as they restacked their books and papers. Then footsteps came up closer and plop! The person dropped down in the seat directly behind Jan. The bus began to move.

Where's Mark Fury? Jan suddenly thought.

Jan looked around at the students in front of him. He could see the other teenagers Mark had been talking to earlier, but not Mark himself. Jan could feel the hairs on the back of his neck stand up. His breaths became deeper as his eyes made a second sweep of everyone in front.

"Well, well. If it isn't the scrawny sissy-boy," came the whispering voice from behind him. "How come you didn't save me the seat next to you, huh? Are you scared of being with guys? I thought guys like you liked other guys."

Again Jan's soul sank within. His mind went blank. The tingling sensation came back to his arms and chest. He went into statue mode.

Jan stared straight ahead. His eyes caught the mirror at the front of the bus. The bus driver looked up at it about the same time, checking all the students. Jan wanted to get his attention somehow. As their eyes met in the mirror, however, Mark nodded from behind and gave the driver a quick wave. The bus driver smiled and then fixed his eyes on the road again.

Suddenly Jan felt the grip of cold fingers on the back of his neck. Jan's whole body shivered and his shoulders shot in an effort to protect his neck. Trying not to make a scene, Jan pressed his head back to to try to squeeze Mark's hands out.

"Maybe you and I should get together after school, Jan," came the whisper again. "You know. Duke it out. You can show me how much of a man you are. Oops. That's right, you're not one."

Jan shivered at Mark's icy touch.

"Still, I think it would be fun. You and me after school, okay?"

Pleadingly, Jan looked up at the mirror again. Mark followed his lead and smiled. The driver just sipped some coffee and watched the road.

"Say, 'yes,' Sissy-boy."

Jan clamped down on his teeth and his lips formed a grimace.

"Say it."

The bus curved into the high school parking lot. Everyone on the bus started to lean into the turn. That was when Jan put his weight into it. Jan's neck slipped through Mark's fingers as his body fell sideways. Mark's nails scratched his neck a little before letting go, but Jan felt free again.

Mark tried to stand up slightly and reach over Jan's seat. Fortunately, the force of the turn kept him off balance. He struck the metal frame around Jan's seat and fell backward. The bus screeched to a stop and made a puffing sound at the south end of the long brick structure with multiple entryways.

While Jan was still lying on the seat, Mark stood up. He looked down at Jan with narrowed eyes. Then he looked toward the front of the bus. Suddenly, his face loosened and a smile arose. Mark began walking forward.

Jan sat up to see the driver watching the students in the mirror again. That must have scared Mark off for the moment. Jan watched as Mark made his way down the aisle behind all the other kids. As he reached the front of the bus, Mark patted the bus driver on the shoulder and said something Jan couldn't quite hear. The bus driver smiled at Mark and nodded.

As Mark turned toward the door, Jan scooped up his books. He watched out the window carefully as Mark continued his walk into the building. Again Jan took a deep breath. Then he walked up toward to the bus driver also.

"You doing okay, son?" asked the driver.

"Yeah. I'm okay."

"Your friend said he was a little worried about you. Didn't think you were feeling well."

"I'm okay." Jan turned away from the driver and stepped out the door.

Other students were pouring into the building from other buses, smiling and laughing. They dashed past him to get into the warm building as quickly as they could, occasionally bumping into him or cutting in front of him, in their frenzy to get inside. He felt more like an obstacle for them rather than a fellow human being.

Jan trudged his way into the brick structure and down some

75

hallways to his locker. Steve and Jenny were nowhere in sight now. Throwing his coat into his locker, he grabbed his history book and headed toward Mr. Gray's class. Waves of students passed him in both directions. His face looked downward at the speckled floor guiding him to his first class. Somehow, it felt more like guidance toward his execution. Nothing in him wanted to keep going. The locker-filled hallways seemed endless today.

Suddenly, a hand grabbed his shoulder. He felt his eyes go wide. All he could think of was that it wasn't the end of the school day yet.

"Jan."

He turned slowly, his hands in protective mode. But instead of the face of Mark Fury, it was Mr. Guideron. His eyes and muscles relaxed.

"Are you okay, Jan? You don't look well."

"Yeah. I'm fine, Mr. Guideron." He looked back down at the speckled floor. The dark red spots seemed to resemble bloodstains now.

"You're very pale. And what's that on your neck."

Immediately, Jan's hand shot up and touched the spot on his neck where Mark had held him. There was a scratch there. It had happened when he leaned away from Mark on the bus.

"Nothing. I scratched myself this morning."

"How did you do that – reach around your back? That came from behind you."

"I don't remember. I think it might have happened when I was getting my coat on this morning. The zipper … uh …."

"Jan, is there something you'd like to talk to me about?"

Jan shook his head. "I'm fine."

Mr. Guideron studied Jan's face. "Okay. I'd like to see you at lunch. Why don't you bring your lunch and stop by my office?'

"Okay."

"I'll see you then, Jan." Mr. Guideron turned and walked off in the opposite direction.

Now what? If you fink on Mark Fury during lunch with Mr. Guideron today, it might delay the fight for a day, but he'll take it out on you on the way home some other day. Great choice! So, there's get beat up today or another day. Other guys don't go through this. If you were tough like them, this would never have happened. Why are you such a sissy? What is wrong with you?

Jan could feel the well behind his eyes begin to fill. Students continued to rush by. Jan leaned against a locker and looked up at the ceiling, pretending to examine one of the tiles in the hanging ceiling.

Go away! Go away! He told the tears.

After a few seconds, the pool of water did subside. Jan returned to his walk toward Mr. Gray's Modern U.S. History class. Once inside the room, he plopped down on the cold desk chair, pressing his back against the seat and leaning his head back momentarily. Closing his eyes, he took some deep breaths.

Jan took notes throughout the hour and when Mr. Gray got off subject, he sketched pictures in the margins. That became his pattern in most of his classes that day. Focus on what he had to do.

Gym class, however, was different. Mark Fury leered at him the whole hour. Jan's stomach tossed and turned even more. About 15 minutes into class, he told coach he wasn't feeling well and asked if he could sit down. Coach agreed. Even then, Mark never stopped giving him looks.

When Coach called everyone back to the locker room, Jan lingered a little longer on the bleachers. No one would miss him. Maybe Barry, but he was into talking with some other guys today.

He watched the clock tick away. Second by second. Moving his palms gently over his abdomen, he took a few deep breaths. He knew he couldn't wait there long. With his stomach feeling as it was, he knew he'd be needing to use the restroom. It would probably be the first of many trips today. Once his intestines went into this mode, they became unpredictable. He might need to use the restroom twice in five minutes at times.

Slowly, he stood up. Folding his arms and pressing them into his gut, he made his way down the steps, one at a time. His head felt kind of odd too. Just sort of fuzzy. The large empty gym echoed each footstep.

Stepping cautiously, he made his way to the locker room door and headed down the long hallway. Pressure in his lower abdomen grew. He veered off into the restroom area and closed a stall door behind him. No sooner had he sat down, then it felt like every meal over the last 24 hours flowed right out of him. A feeling of exhaustion soon followed. He thought he could hear the other guys talking out by the lockers, but their words didn't seem to have meaning. In the stall, he felt cut off from everything and everyone. His aching stomach and overall weakness became his world.

After about five minutes of nothing more happening, he raised himself up. He still felt weak and a little unsteady. Adjusting his gym shorts, he walked out into the mostly empty locker area. Only a handful of guys finished dressing there.

Jan felt exhausted but knew he should still take a shower. His grades in gym were probably bad enough by this time in the semester. So, he stripped down, wrapped a towel around his waist and walked into the showers. Hanging the towel up on a hook, he walked over to the nearest shower head and turned it on.

The warm water actually felt nice as it enfolded him in a wet hug. It appeared to even calm his stomach some. If he could only stay under this for like a half-hour.

"Richards."

The voice startled him and he dropped the soap. Jan turned around quickly to see Mark Fury leering at him from the doorway. Jan wanted to cover himself or turn back away from Mark, but showing embarrassment was a sign of weakness for guys. So, he stood there vulnerable and weak.

"Did I scare you, Sissy-boy? Don't forget – after school." He looked at Jan's body and snickered.

"Fury, is that you mumbling? Ain't you got a class coming up?" came Coach's voice from his office in the next room.

"Sorry, Coach. Just checking up Richards. He still doesn't look good."

"Oh, yeah?"

Jan heard the coach's chair get pushed back. Mark immediately left. Then, Coach stepped into the doorway and stared into Jan's face.

"You okay, Jan? You're looking a paler than you did earlier."

"It's still my stomach, Coach."

"You got medication for that?"

"I'll … be okay."

"You may want to stop by the front office and have the secretary take a quick look."

"Okay."

Coach turned and walked away as if he failed to notice Jan had been standing naked in front of him with all his imperfections. Feeling safe again, Jan turned back around. A quick rinse off and Jan grabbed his towel again. As he began dressing, he heard the bell go off down the hallway. Fortunately that signaled lunch.

Finishing dressing, Jan walked slowly down to the cafeteria. His stomach felt a little better, but still did not feel like much for lunch. So, he just grabbed a chocolate-covered wafer cookie to eat. Scanning the cafeteria, he spotted a girl reading a book with a few open seats around her in the back corner. He made his way over to her and sat down. She didn't even glance over at him. Thank God for readers.

Slowly munching on his cookie, Jan pondered the situation and forgot about his appointment with Mr. Guideron. He actually could go to the office because of sickness. Coach was right. They could call his mom to pick him up. That would avoid Mark at the end of the day. However, he really wanted to go to drawing class.

Another option was to stay after school long enough so he would have to take a later bus back to the middle school. That would probably avoid Mark too. Even if he missed the later bus because he saw Mark get on it, he could still call his mom to pick him up when she got out of work.

Two possible ways out. His stomach was beginning to settle down already. Chances were he'd still have to eat something gentle and bland like Cream of Wheat for supper tonight, but at least his stomach wasn't aching as bad as it had been.

* * * * *

Drawing class had become the pinnacle of school life for Jan. The teacher, Mr. Darragh, allowed students to draw whatever they desired. Jan had been working on a drawing of David facing Goliath. It had been Pastor Enoch's suggestion actually. He had told Jan he needed some artwork for a wall in his office. If Jan would draw it for him, he would get it framed.

Jan had a few books on famous sculptures next to him on the art table to get the muscles to look just right. In his drawing, David was standing tall and confident, lean and lithe, in typical, loose biblical garb, pulling his slingshot taunt. Meanwhile, Goliath was charging at him in full armor with a muscular body resembling the Incredible Hulk, with bulging muscles.

Jan had also found a picture of the Valley of Elah where the battle actually took place in an encyclopedia at the library. The photo made this valley look pretty flat. However the unusual hill surrounding it on each side looked like several hills God had smooshed together. Hills carried on for miles, like the constant waves on a windy day at the beach.

Over the past few days, various aspects of the drawing had to be erased and redrawn several times before Jan thought it looked right. That had taken days. There were a couple of times Jan gave up. In the end, however, he kept coming back to it and redrawing.

He sat at the large, wooden table with five other people, mostly girls. They included male anatomy experts, Jill and Karen, from history class who were keeping their most recent copy of Playgirl out of sight. They always looked around the room, especially at guys, whispered to each other, and giggled. Sometimes they did it with Jan too. It made him wonder what they knew. Thankfully, they were the only questionable aspect of drawing class. Most of the time, Jan could ignore what they were doing by concentrating on his artwork.

There also sat a pair of sisters at the table. Jan was never sure if they were really drawing or just scribbling. They mostly played music on their cassette player and talked. The last student at the table everyone called "Ace." He seemed dedicated to art as well. Ace was a junior but sometimes he and Jan talked together about art and shared drawings for short periods of time.

On this day though, the memory of Mark's threat kept coming back into Jan's head. Jan's stomach tossed and turned more than ever as the end of the school day approached. So, he took a deep breath and put his focus on his artwork. He stared at the penciled line on the paper. Just don't think about Mark, he told himself. Concentrate on the drawing. Look at David.

Before him lay the penciled sketch of the young, teenage hero against the nine-foot-tall enemy warrior. Jan could just see the ground shaking beneath Goliath's feet as he dashed toward David. But David was unafraid, a real man, standing in defiance of the giant who was out to destroy him.

Jan drew a felt marker from his pocket. As he applied the marker to the penciled lines, the drawing came to life. David gained clarity and determination with each stroke. Goliath grew more powerful and menacing.

The sudden bell ringing startled Jan. Nothing inside him wanted to hear that sound – like the bell before a boxing match. Most others scrambled to pick up their supplies, but Jan continued inking his artwork. As they hurried out the art door, he asked Mr. Darragh if he could stay a few more minutes to finish up. Mr. Darragh smiled gently and said, "Sure." Jan could feel his stomach flip-flopping more as he returned to his seat.

What if this doesn't work? he wondered. Mark seemed so intent today. He might wait for Jan as long as he took. Mark could have his mom pick him up too if he stayed past the later bus while waiting for Jan. And when did the office staff leave? What if they left before Jan's and Mark's moms picked them up? Jan and Mark would be in the school alone together. Then, what?

The acid in his stomach now bubbled up like lava in a volcano.

Concentrate on your drawing, Jan told himself. So, he took out his pencil again and retraced lines already on the paper. Guilt welled up inside as he sketched. He felt like he was cheating. Men were supposed to be people of their word. Here he was hiding in a classroom to stay away from a bully.

The tingling sensation returned to his arms and chest. With it came the negative voice again.

You're being a sissy. A real man would fight Mark Fury.

But Jan knew he wouldn't win. He couldn't win. Jan's hand began to shake. The pencil fell out of his hand onto the wood table. Bringing his hands together, he placed his head in them.

"Jan, are you okay, buddy?" asked Mr. Darragh.

He wanted to say yes, but the word would not form. Mr. Darragh walked over and put his arm on Jan's shoulder. "You don't look well, Jan. I think we should take a walk down to the office."

Jan nodded.

Mr. Darragh helped Jan pick up his books and supplies. Gently, he helped him up out of the chair. By this point, Jan's stomach bubbled continuously. Soon he'd be needing to go to the restroom.

Mr. Darragh walked beside Jan all the way down the hallway. They passed through the bright cafeteria and out the doors and into the main hallway. The office stood directly in front of them, along with the main doors to the school. And to the right side of the main doors, Mark Fury rested against the brick wall, patiently waiting.

As Mark realized who Mr. Darraugh was helping into the office, his expression changed. Scrutiny became blazing anger. Mark crossed his arms and narrowed his eyes at Jan. Jan dropped his chin down to his chest and looked at the floor.

"You okay, man? You don't feel like you're gonna pass out, do you?" Mr. Darragh asked.

Jan looked up again. He caught one last glimpse of Mark as they turned into the office doorway. He had escaped a fight with Mark this time. Obviously, Mark was taking a mental raincheck for now.

Sissy. Sissy-boy. You've had it now.

Afraid We Are Not

Chapter 10

The latest episode of abdominal sickness kept Jan out of school for almost two weeks. He still got up and got dressed each day, however his stomach felt like it was filled with bubbling, hot grease. Just getting up and walking to the kitchen exhausted him for the first few days.

Jan's diet consisted of Cream of Wheat, sugar-cinnamon toast, and dishes of peaches on most days. He could have some 7-Up as well. Virtually, anything else upset his stomach.

Recovery wasn't all bad, however. It gave him a sense of peace again. No more dodging the bullies for a while. He reread all of his Phantom comic books and sketched out pictures of various newspaper comic characters in a new art journal his mom had bought for him to keep busy. It was fun drawing Snoopy, Hagar the Horrible, and a few others. He discovered Dondi was the easiest adventure strip character to draw; Brenda Starr, the most difficult. Something about her artist's style made it hard to duplicate.

Meanwhile, in the newspapers, the Phantom had finally caught up with everyone involved in stealing the Star of Bangalla. Det. Dick Tracy had captured the all-female gang, except for their leader, Lispy, who was on the lam. Honeymooning Brenda Starr was kidnapped briefly but then freed by a pair of child stowaways on the ship.

Steve came to see Jan several times after school while he was stuck at home, once with Jenny. That time, Steve brought him a copy of "The Phantom and the Assassins," a novel featuring his favorite hero.

"Thought you might be getting tired of rereading your old comics," Steve said. "I knew you liked the Phantom."

"Where did you find it?!" Jan's eyes brightened. "I was looking for it last year."

"They still had a copy behind some other books down in the paperback racks at Decker's. I was looking for a cowboy book for my dad and ran across it."

Meanwhile, Jenny walked around the brown and tan room and looked at all Jan's drawings on the walls. She even asked questions about them and made comments about the people. She said she thought she could identify the people from Jan's drawings if she saw them walking down the street. The drawings were that good.

"I knew you loved to draw, Jan, but I had no idea you were this talented," Jenny said.

Jan blushed. "Thanks."

The friends spent time talking, mostly about school. Jan's friends caught him up on all that was happening. Communications and English teachers Forrest, DePlume, MacEthain, and Steward were creating Gunwale's first creative writing and speech contest with a grand prize of $50. The boys basketball team had won the game against their toughest opponents, St. Ignace. Jenny knew what couples were still going together and which ones had broken up. Between the two of them, Jan came up to speed up on just about everything he had missed.

As they prepared to leave, Jenny walked up to Jan and surrounded him in her arms. For a moment, he felt numb. Then, he realized he needed to place his arms around her as well. Despite the fact she was wearing her thick parka, he could feel a person inside. A real person, not just padding. As they held each other briefly, he could swear energy passed from her to him and any remaining fear passed out of his body. Jenny smiled back at him as if nothing had happened while she pulled away. Once again, Jan's body went into a statue state as he released her and attempted to smile back. What was he supposed to do after a girl hugged him?

When the smooching couple left, Jan put on his parka and shoes to step outside to get the newspaper. The short walk didn't tire him out as he thought. That meant his days away from school would soon be at their end. He just tried not to think about Mark Fury or the Weasel. Usually, the first few days returning to school after an episode, teachers kept somewhat of a watch on Jan, because he would still be slightly weak. Their watchfulness should prevent him from having to dodge the bullies again for a while.

* * * * *

When he returned to school, the weather had begun to warm up again. March brought in temperatures in the 40s. Snowbanks began to shrink a little. Most of his teachers gave him a couple weeks to get caught up on what he had missed during his absence. Of course, there would be nothing for gym. In fact, Jan's doctor was advised him to take another week off of physical activity to recover his endurance. In art, he just kept working on his drawing of David and Goliath. He had to make up a speech for Mr. Steward's public speaking class. In Borderlines of Reality, Mr. Forrest just said he just needed to catch up reading in "The Hobbit." Meteorology, health, and history just required some reading and a few worksheets to fill out.

He saw Mr. Guideron in the halls often over those days. The counselor constantly asked how he was feeling. Seeing the counselor so often in the halls seemed a little odd. Jan wondered if Mr. Guideron wasn't keeping a special eye on him.

The days felt like a fresh start to his sophomore year once again. Mark Fury gave him a narrow-eyed, evil smile a couple of times, but nothing worse than that. He kept his distance most of the time.

On Friday, however, life took another turn. Jan sat in Mr. Sobear's biology class. They had just finished a movie on the life of the African lion. Some of the girls in class were still upset by a scene of the lion taking down and devouring a zebra.

"Survival of the fittest is what life is about," the teacher with wavy but slicked-back, blond hair and glasses began. "I know that may bother some of you who like to romanticize life, but these are the facts. It is the most fit in nature who survive and carry on their species. The strong who survive. Others are just food."

"That seems cruel," one girl commented.

"No one ever said nature is kind. She always chooses the strong over the weak."

A senior from the football team who sat in front of Jan quickly spoke up. "So, what your saying is the athletes will succeed in this world. The rest of these chumps in here are just somebody's food."

The athletes in the class all broke out in cheers and laughter. The girls and the boys from band and drama club all booed and stuck their tongues out. In the midst of the disruption, the senior in front of Jan bent his head backward and looked at Jan upside-down.

"Hello, food," he said with a wide grin.

"Even food has its purpose though," Mr. Sobear corrected. "The lion couldn't survive without the zebra being there to eat."

Jan could feel his stomach beginning to react again. Bubbling and churning started once more. He could feel breakfast making its way toward the exit.

You're so sensitive, Sissy. The negative voice pounced again. *Sissy-boy.*

Jan raised his hand and asked for a restroom pass. It would be better to be proactive in this case. Mr. Sobear handed it over.

As Jan walked out, the senior yelled up at the teacher. "That was for the restroom marked 'Weak,' right, Mr. Sobear?"

Jan closed the door before an answer came. He sighed as he made his way down the long hall. It was one time Jan hoped his stomach episode might last a while. Like the rest of the class time. As he rounded a corner, he nearly bumped shoulders with another student.

Mark Fury stopped and stared back at him, revealing one of his evil smirks. Jan stopped too. Then Mark glanced around. All was quiet except for some typing coming from the school office about 50 feet away. The restroom sat only a short distance from the office, but once the restroom door closed, anything could happen. It seemed like those were the most sound-proof rooms in the whole building. Although there were private toilets inside for teachers and staff, it was a rare day when either would be seen going into them.

Mark's mouth suddenly became a straight line and he nodded for Jan to move ahead. Cautiously, Jan took a couple of steps forward. Once he had his back to Mark, he heard Mark take steps too, right behind him. Jan stopped and turned. Mark raised his eyebrows innocently.

"You can go ahead, Mark."

"Naw, that's all right, Jan. Little boys go first."

The tingling feeling came back into his chest and arms as Jan backed against the lockers behind him. If they both used the restroom at the same time, Jan knew what would happen now. He could tell by the tone of Mark's voice. He didn't need any more insults about his masculinity right now. Again the negative voice spoke up.

Sissy. Sissy-boy.

"You probably need it quicker than I do. Go ahead," Jan said pressing his back further against the lockers.

Mark slowly walked up to Jan. He smiled again, inches from him.

"I haven't forgotten, Richards. We're still going to do this. Maybe after school today," Mark whispered.

Mark stared at him through those narrowed eyes again.

"You can play sick little momma's boy all you want. I'm still going to womp your butt."

Jan could feel the hot grease developing in his stomach again. Mark's right hand came up. His index finger began poking at Jan's chest.

"I'll be waiting for you, Sissy-boy."

No sooner had Mark finished the last word than footsteps came to be heard coming down from the other end of the hall. It was Mr.

Guideron. He was on his way toward them from the other direction. His eyes seemed to suddenly focus on Mark. Immediately, Mark stepped back. His hand suddenly became an open palm and he patted Jan's shoulder.

In a louder than usual voice, he said, "Glad to hear your feeling better, Jan."

Mark quickly turned and strutted off to the bathroom, shouting before going in, "Hey, Mr. Guideron."

Jan breathed out a truckload of air as Mr. Guideron walked over to him.

"Are you okay, Jan? Are you having any problems?" he asked glancing at the men's room.

"I'm okay now. I mean, I'm okay."

"I am available to talk right now if you need me."

Jan shook his head and stared at the ground. "It's okay. I'm fine."

"All right. If you need me I'm here."

Slowly Mr. Guideron backtracked toward the office. Jan plodded over to the restroom door and waited outside. The counselor looked back once more before entering the office. Jan stared at the floor.

Moments later, the men's room door burst open and Mark strutted out, looking pleased with himself. Seeing Jan, he stopped and turned.

"Good morning, Mark." Mr. Guideron's voice seemed to echo in the hall as he stood in the office doorway.

Mark nodded, waved at Mr. Guideron, and walked off. Jan looked over at his counselor and the corners of his mouth rose slightly. He nodded back at Jan. Then, the two turned and walked in their separate ways. Already Jan's stomach seemed to be settling down.

Gym class followed. With Jan still trying to get all his strength back, he watched the class from the bleachers while catching up on the school he had missed while being sick. It also kept him away from Mark, who still stared at him through narrow eyes at times. Fortunately, his seat in the bleachers made it easy to ignore Mark. Since Jan wasn't playing, he didn't need to use the locker room either. Jan waited in the same spot until everyone left to change clothes. Once the bell rang and

Mark headed down the hallway, he would leave too. All went as planned.

Throughout the rest of the day, he avoided looking Mark in the eyes whenever he spotted him walking down the hall among the other students between classes. By the end of the day, Jan's stomach felt just about back to normal.

Jan held his books and looked into his locker one last time. His art journal he had brought to school was missing. The last time he saw it was in drawing class. Turning back from where he had just come, Jan hurried through waves of people, all rushing in the opposite direction toward him. Reaching the office, he turned left, crossing through the cafeteria, passing by the auditorium doors, through some double doors, he entered the arts wing of the school. Just past the home economics room and the student-run restaurant, where students served lunch to interested students and teachers, stood the art room.

Jan swung into the art room. It was empty. Mr. Darragh must be off somewhere. He looked over at his table to the right. No art journal. Immediately he walked over to his chair. Nothing on the chair or under it. Where could it be? He looked at the three other large wooden tables. All stood bare. Next, he studied at the cabinets and countertops surrounding the room. Still no notebook.

He ran over to Mr. Darragh's desk. There it was – right on top. He breathed a sigh of relief, then scooped it up. He didn't know if he could make it back to the other end of the school in time to catch the first bus or not.

Jan dashed out the door. Passing another hallway to his left, he caught, out of the corner of his eye, another figure coming his way. As he passed the student restaurant, he took note of his straining lungs and wondered if he might need his inhaler again. Then, something latched onto his shoulders and jerked him backward. His back slammed into the wall. Books crashed onto the floor. Mark Fury stepped in front of him.

"Trying to run away before I got out of shop class, aren't you, Sissy-boy?"

"I forgot something in the art room."

"What did you tell Mr. Guideron?"

"Nothing."

"Are you sure?"

"Yes. I just want to catch the bus."

"Too bad, 'cause you're not going to be able to. Remember, you owe me a dukin' contest."

"I don't want to fight you, Mark."

Mark grabbed ahold of Jan's shirt and twisted it in his fist. "That's because you're a sissy. Sissies are too scared to fight. Boy on the outside, girl on the inside. And a very little boy at that."

Mark's narrowed eyes stared into Jan's. They seemed to be able to see what was going on in his mind. Jan could feel his soul beginning to cower in a corner deep inside him. His body went into statue mode again. He summoned up all his strength, but water began to gather in his eyes. Not the sissy tears. Not the sissy tears.

Mark pressed his fist hard against Jan's chest.

"Every day, I tell you, Sissy-boy ...."

Suddenly, the sound of a metal mechanism engaging stopped the conversation. Mark's hand released Jan's shirt. The hall doors burst open and Mr. Guideron stepped through. He grabbed Mark's shoulder and ripped him away from Jan in a quick jerk.

"Whoa, Mr. Guideron, Jan and I were just having a discussion," Mark quickly said.

"That's not the way it sounded to me."

"Well, it was getting a little heated, but I wouldn't have let it go too far, sir."

Jan just stared, not knowing what to say.

"Shut up, Mark. I heard your discussion from the other side of those doors. We are taking a walk down to the counseling office."

Mr. Guideron nodded at Jan to follow. The counselor steered Mark by the back of the neck and pointed him toward the counseling office. Jan followed close behind them. As they entered the waiting area, Mr. Guideron guided Mark into one private office, told him he'd be back, and closed the door.

"Come on, Jan," he said, motioning him into another private office. Jan sat down.

"I heard what Mark was saying. This has been going on for quite a while, hasn't it?"

Jan felt his face flush. He stared down at the carpeted floor and nodded.

"I had a feeling …." the counselor muttered. "Okay, Jan. Wait here. I am going to talk to Mr. Stone about the situation and we'll discuss how to deal with Mark's behavior."

As he walked away, Mr. Guideron turned to his secretary. "Mr. Fury is not to leave that office until I return. I don't care if his kidneys are about to explode. He stays put."

The wide-eyed secretary nodded. Then, Mr. Guideron stepped out of the counseling office.

The counseling office and the school offices had two different entryways, but the rooms butted up against each other. Although the walls were concrete block, when all was silent it was possible to hear conversation on the other side of the wall. After a couple of minutes, Jan heard the door to the principal's office open in the room behind him.

"Mr. Stone, I have a boy in my office who's being bullied. What's the policy on dealing with verbal abuse?" asked Mr. Guideron.

"Verbal abuse? You mean some other kid is calling him names? Kids are always doing that. Especially boys. You'd have to be awfully thin-skinned to let that bother ya."

"We are not talking about a one-time event here. This has likely been going on for some time."

"Did the bully ever hit him or kick him?"

"No."

Mr. Guideron must have forgotten about the scratch this morning, Jan thought.

"Then, no one can prove what really happened. It's one kid's word against another. We don't mess with that. There's not enough staff to police each kid's conversations."

"I heard what he said this time."

"Doesn't matter, Guideron. We can't prove words. Hitting and kicking leave marks. We can prove those. Words don't leave marks on people. If the other kid's parents decide to sue us, we'd have nothing to stand on."

"So, what is the victim supposed to do?"

"Stop being so blasted sensitive. What is he some kind of sissy?"

Sissy. Sissy-boy. Fragile, scrawny Sissy-boy.

Again Jan's soul became weak-kneed.

"Where is this boy's father in all this, Guideron? Didn't he ever teach him how to fight?"

"His father is dead."

"Is this that Richards boy?"

"Yes."

"He is a waste of time. Cowardice runs in his family."

"What?"

"I said, cowardice runs in his family."

"What do you mean?"

"His uncle couldn't hack it during World War II. Lost his head in the middle of battle and ran off. Jan Richard's father's army unit was one of the first on the scene on D-Day. His whole platoon was killed off. Only he survived. What does that tell you?"

"I don't know. That he was lucky?"

"No! He was obviously a coward too. Ran off and hid somewhere until after the fighting was over."

"How do you know this? Were you there?"

"No. But just about everyone in town has heard that story. Even his old girlfriend, Eleanor Fury, has said he used to act fearful around her. And she sits on our school board."

You're from a whole family of cowards, Sissy-boy. It's in your genes. Everybody in town knows what you are.

Dad? Jan thought. That can't be true.

"You're telling me you're making a decision on a boy's future

93

based on gossip?"

"Boys like him have no future. He's like that Quarry boy we had in here several years ago. Couldn't handle the outside world and took his own life. That's the way life thins out the pack, You know, survival of the fittest."

"Then, what am I supposed to tell Jan Richards to do?"

"Next time that bully says something, hit him with all he's got."

"And if a fight breaks out, then what?"

"You know what comes after that. They both get suspended."

"That's your answer – punish the victim?"

"Those are the rules, Mr. Guideron. I am paid to uphold the rules of this school district."

"What do I tell Jan, Mr. Stone?"

"You tell that sissy to toughen up. Grow some genitals. In this world, men need to be tough to make it."

Sissy. Sissy-boy. Everyone knows what you are. They talk about you behind your back. What Mark Fury tells you is all true.

Everything inside Jan felt like it was breaking apart, like dried up clay soil. No soul. No emotion. Just complete emptiness inside. If someone were to poke him, he felt like his body would just crumble to dust on the chair and floor.

He heard the door in Mr. Stone's office close. The principal cussed quietly. Then total silence took over. Within a couple of minutes, Mr. Guideron came back into the counseling office. Immediately, he walked briskly into the office where Mark was being held. The door shut. Even though the talk was muffled, Jan could still hear the conversation.

"We are letting you off with a warning this time, Mark. But I don't ever want to see you hassling Jan Richards again. Is that understood?"

"Jan was just confused, Mr. Guideron. I don't think he understood what I was saying."

Mr. Guideron shot back with a reference to cow manure.

"I heard what you said to him, Mark. You're not fooling me. Whenever you are around Jan from now on, you keep your mouth shut.

Now, get out."

The door opened. Jan watched as Mark strutted out of the room. He glanced over at Jan and smiled with his head held high. Mr. Guideron came into Jan's room looking somewhat perplexed. He cast a forced smile at Jan.

"I have given Mark Fury a warning. If he ever bothers you again, calls you names, whatever, you come and talk to me."

Jan accepted the advice and picked up his things. He knew there was nothing Mr. Guideron could really do. The principal was in charge of punishment. Perhaps Mr. Guideron's words would make Mark a little more cautious for a while. Eventually, Mark would figure out the counselor couldn't carry through on any threats he made. Then what?

It seemed Jan and Mark were on a collision course. Fighting would be the end result. And everyone knew when you put a sissy and a tough guy into a fight who would come out the winner.

The bus ride back to the middle school in town remained quiet. Jan and Mark sat at different ends of the bus. Neither said a word nor looked at each other in the eye. As an added precaution though, Jan let Mark get off first and walk down Chestnut Street about a block ahead before he followed.

The wind blew his thin, carrot-colored hairs as he walked down the dry pavement toward the main street. Since he knew the growing tension between Mark and him had been put on hold, his mind concentrated on the story about his father.

Did Sue know? Had Sue heard the story? She never mentioned it and it would be hard to keep something that controversial to herself. The story made no sense, however. How could Dad have been a coward? Did that mean I inherited being a sissy? No, Dad never showed signs of being afraid of anything. He was always calm in difficult situations.

Sissy. Sissy-boy.

Stop! Stop! Stop! he told the negative voice.

Jan needed to talk to Sue about Dad. Maybe when she came home tonight, before they went to bed he could. He had to concentrate on that problem. But once again, the voice pushed its way into his thoughts.

Sissy-boy. Why didn't you fight Mark?

I wouldn't have won anyway. I'm not tough enough. Even Dad said so.

You're such a sissy. Sissy-boy.

Stop! Stop! Jan's mind shouted.

When Jan arrived home, he heard Sue back in her bedroom off the kitchen for a change. She was talking to someone too. He listened quietly to see he could identify the voice.

"You are so lucky to have your own room," the other feminine voice said. "I hate sharing mine with my sisters."

The voice appeared to be that of Sue's hippy friend, Heidi. She was the most unique of all Sue's friends. Dressed with a headband and a jean jacket filled with flower patches, she looked like she had been frozen in time since the late '60s and recently thawed out.

But Heidi was unquestionably an artist. She mostly created necklaces and bracelets with beads and macrame. She had given Sue some of her creations as gifts. But her talent went beyond just crafts. Jan had seen some of her drawings in a sketchbook she sometimes carried and some paintings she had created in art class. Her artwork was amazing. Jan admired her work.

Most of the time, Heidi was very mellow. Her mood ring was in a constant state of green. She seemed to float beside her other friends rather than walk. All her actions seemed to flow gently to a song only she could hear.

Even so, there seemed to be a dark side to Heidi. Her jean jacket had a smokey odor most of the time. The smell wasn't cigarettes though. Jan figured it was probably marijuana. Sue and other girls often called her what sounded like "Hei" for short. But he was pretty sure her nickname was meant to be "High."

Heidi had only sisters in her family. There were five.

"I have to share my bedroom with Kelli and Cheryl," he heard her say now.

"I don't know. Sometimes I wish I had a sister," Sue replied.

"Consider yourself lucky. Mine are always uptight."

"Really?"

"Yeah. I'd like to substitute one of my cigarettes for theirs sometime. Mellow them out for a while."

Both girls laughed.

"Are you still going out with Terry Nelson?" Sue asked.

"I was. I don't think I will anymore though. He seems to only want one thing.

"Don't you hate it when guys treat girls that way."

"I'll say. I like to get out and do stuff. Seems like around here all guys are like Terry."

"I can't wait to go to college where they are more mature."

"You think so?"

"That's what I've heard. This older cousin of mine goes to State. She says guys there are more mature, especially when they get to be juniors and seniors. She's dating this senior guy and says he always brings her flowers."

"I like flowers," Heidi said and then giggled, realizing the obviousness of her statement.

"I'm just looking for a guy whose, not a chauvinist. He still opens doors for me and pays for meals, but treats me like an equal. He needs to be very brave. He should have straight teeth, be nicely groomed, kind of muscular without looking like a weight lifter, and lots of chest hair."

"I've decided I'm going to order mine from a catalog."

"Oh, yeah. I'm sure."

"Look."

Jan could hear something like the slick cover of a magazine being pulled out from other books.

"That's no catalog! Where did you get that?"

"Well, this is my catalog. It's just for women. Guys have all kinds of their own where they compare those girls' bodies to ours. We should be able to do the same. Look at the guys in these pictures."

It must be a Playgirl, Jan concluded.

"We gotta be careful. Can't let my mom see that. She'd have a cow."

Jan didn't need to hear more. He knew what they were looking at. Again, his soul began to weaken. *Are all girls like this? If they are, I'm truly a hopeless case.* Jan slowly turned and shuffled off to the living room and then into his bedroom. He might as well forget about ever dating. He crashed down onto his bed, on his stomach, and gripped the sides tightly. *Where did I go wrong? God must really be ashamed of me. I must be His most horrible disappointment.*

Sissy-boy, you're never going to be good enough for anyone. Even the principal thought there was something wrong with your body. You heard Sue and Heidi. You will never be a man. Not what they are looking for. What any girl wants.

Stop.

You messed up somewhere, Sissy-boy. You probably ran from Mark Fury too many times when you were younger. That's probably what made you a sissy. You failed. That's why your dad left. He couldn't stand what you were becoming. He didn't want a sissy for a son.

The wells in his eyes began to refill. This time he didn't fight it. He just surrendered. Because that is what a sissy does. He stayed there on his bed until his mom called him for supper. He decided against talking to Sue about Dad.

Chapter 11

After finishing his homework that night and being unable to sketch anything, Jan decided to watch TV with his mom. She wanted to watch some new TV drama called "Family." Jan wasn't keen on dramas, but tonight it beat being alone in his room. Watching TV could keep the negative voice at bay also.

Not far into the program, it seemed like all the characters were arguing with someone else. The best characters were the brother and the younger sister, who seemed to get along well. Unlike Jan and Sue who mostly stayed out of each other's way.

The brother was told to pick up his little sister from school. Evidently, she had gotten into a fight with another girl. It didn't say what her age was on the show, but she only looked like 13, at most. She told him another girl called her a shrimp. Turned out his sister was being teased about her development and worried she wasn't developing fast enough. Her brother even used the word "flat-chested." On a TV show! Jan couldn't even look at his mom as the characters were talking about this stuff. He sank back into the chair, half wishing he would be absorbed by the upholstery.

Then, the TV brother reassured his younger sister everyone makes it through puberty. No one stops in the middle and is left behind.

Eventually, everyone catches up. Even though the whole scene was kind of embarrassing, there was something of a release inside Jan at the same time. Girls actually worried about being "freaks" in their bodies too? They always seemed so confident to Jan. At least, the ones he heard talking.

"You'll catch up." Jan smiled just a little recalling the brother's words as he climbed into bed. Still, he had overheard stories from other guys when they were in groups a couple of years back. Stories of boys who never became real men. So, which was really true? And what if he was an exception?

* * * * *

On Wednesday, Jan worked beside Pastor Enoch in the narthex of the church again. The pastor was teaching Jan about sanding down some of the end pieces for the shelves. He would scrub for a while and then slowly follow the curve of the area with his fingertips. The pastor would even close his eyes as he guided his fingers along. Only after his fingers found a flaw would he open his eyes to take a look at it.

"Pastor, how did you learn about carpentry?" Jan asked, sanding another piece.

"Like all skills, someone had to teach me. I had this one friend in high school, Jim Zimmermann. He worked on projects all the time in his parents' garage. He taught me about it. Jim was a great guy – very tall, very quiet, and a little awkward. He was what people referred to as a gentle giant. And he could do amazing things with wood and a few tools.

"But you know what I remember most about Jim? One day the basketball coach approached him and asked him to try out for the basketball team. Jim thought he was crazy. He tried to explain to the coach, he wasn't coordinated enough, and he never would be.

"The coach said that didn't matter. He could train him. The coach didn't give up and finally, Jim gave in. That year, the school saw one of its most successful seasons in basketball ever. "

"No joke?"

"No joke. Being tall always made Jim feel awkward. Some of the other guys even gave him a hard time about his awkwardness. But, you see, the coach taught him his height was his strength. The coach made him the team's center. He was the closest player to the basket, so he could score points easier and had more rebounds than any other guy in the district.

"You should have seen him, Jan. Tallest boy in the whole school. When he walked down the halls, he was a whole head taller than everyone else. Even the teachers."

"Really?"

"Oh, yeah. You couldn't miss Jim."

Jan thought for a moment. "Kind of funny how God makes some people so different like that."

A gentle smile came over the pastor's face. "Yes, it is. And, the truth be told, we are all different.

Yet, we are all perfect."

Jan considered the pastor's words with a frown. After moment, he spoke.

"I don't know about that. I mean, people are talking about how some people are better looking than others. And people do have flaws. How can everyone be perfect?"

The pastor chuckled and stroked his beard.

"Because God formed each of us while we were in the womb. It says so right in the Psalms. He gave us certain unique talents to use, whether we choose to use them for His purpose or we simply reject Him. He says in Exodus He made some people blind, deaf, mute. He made my legs this way, Jan."

"Did you ever get teased ... about your legs?"

"Yes. There were many times I did. It hurt, too."

"What did you do?" Jan leaned forward and rested his arm on the table.

"I looked to God for the reason why. Through the Scriptures, I learned God knew us before He even formed us. He thought us up in

His mind. He knew who would dedicate their lives to following Him and those who would reject Him.

"There is something special about those who choose to follow Jesus. Not only were they designed special and given talents, they were given a role to play – a special purpose to use their body, their mind, and their talent for. And what they do for God will be carried on into eternity."

"God really formed my body?"

"Every single part."

"But don't our bodies make us … a certain way?"

"No. Our bodies are created to match the purpose God chose for us, Jan. We're not made the same, because we have a special purpose within God's bigger plan. The only thing you can tell about a person by their physical appearance is what they look like, not who they are, what they are good at or even what they will become."

Jan pulled back away from the table and rested his back against the chair. None of this matched what he had heard. How could your body not make you a sissy? Everyone agreed on that. Didn't they?

"You see, Moses thought his mouth and ability to speak weren't good enough when God called him to be His spokesperson. Yet, He designed Moses' mouth after He knew what Moses' purpose would be. God told him so."

"I wish God would talk to us like that today."

"God can still talk to us today. Usually, He does that through Scripture. When you read the accounts of Moses and others talking to God, He is also speaking to you, Jan."

"So, you're saying you are okay with your legs now?"

"Our enemy, Satan, tries to convince me that my legs are a problem, even now. He does everything to deceive me into thinking that way. When I see men doing things with their legs that I cannot do, sometimes the enemy whispers to me that I am weak and helpless. That I am not really a man at all."

"Really? Even at your age?" Jan regretted that last part as soon as he said it.

But the pastor only laughed. "Absolutely, Jan. That is our weakest point as men – being afraid we are not."

"Afraid we are not," Jan repeated, thinking deeply.

Jan sanded his shelf piece a little more lightly now. Men fearing they weren't men? That made no sense. Jan couldn't think of any guys he knew who had ever said that or even looked like they might be afraid of that. Guys were always ... tough. The only guy who seemed to doubt he was a man was Jan.

There was all that evidence to prove he couldn't be one. Skinny chest and arms. All that. And the fear he felt around other guys. Yet, Pastor just said he felt like he wasn't one sometimes too.

"You know, Jan, most men spend their lives trying to prove they are men because they doubt they are manly enough. They strive for high paying jobs, big bank accounts, sports, cars, or big trucks, beautiful women. All to prove their manliness to themselves. None of their achievements make them feel better permanently though. So, they have to keep doing new things to feel good about themselves.

"It all goes back to the shame we feel as sinners, Jan. Like we talked about before. Shame causes us to know we are not good enough. I believe that feeling we are not man enough starts there and is added to by experiences throughout our lives. Adam let Eve down in the garden. The shame of his failure has become part of the sin package we inherited as men. Instead of turning to God as our Creator to give us what we are missing, however, we try to make ourselves feel better through our own accomplishments."

"But I've never heard guys talk about that."

"You won't. We try to keep up this facade that we are invulnerable. Nothing can hurt us. We don't want other men to know we have that weakness because we fear they will see us as weak and unmanly. Deep inside though we are all hurting and searching for what will make us feel like men."

"Doesn't God want men to be strong? Didn't you say that in one of your sermons?"

"Most men confuse the physical and the spiritual when they look at what the Bible says. When God talks about being strong in the Scriptures, He is not talking about physical strength. He speaks of spiritual strength. Strength to do what's right. Strength to resist doing what is wrong. Lifting weights won't do that. Trusting in God will. Trusting in God produces success and creates confidence. That is, confidence in God."

Jan's mind felt like it was whirling again. "But … how does a guy trust God, I mean, for that kind of stuff?"

"It is all the same trust, Jan, but it spreads over time to affect all areas of our lives. It all starts with the first step of faith. We realize we are sinful creatures and we cannot keep God's commands. Our only hope is trusting in what Jesus did for us on the cross. Out of thankfulness for Jesus' accomplishment, we turn our lives over to God. That is trust or faith. The next step is putting our faith in God on a daily basis. The little things in life as well as the big things.

"God made us as we are. The men who are trying to prove their manhood have forgotten that important point. God created them, male, already. He designed them in the womb. They don't have to prove anything. To anyone. They are already where they need to be physically.

"Jan, I'm a man because God says so. You are a man. God says so."

Suddenly, Jan found himself taking a deep breath. He was tingling again, but not out of fear. His mind felt like it was whirling faster than ever. This time it was not confusion though.

I am a man? And then came the tears. Those silly, sissy tears. Why were they arising now from the bottom of his eyes? Of all times for this to happen! Should he cover his face? Should he go to the restroom?

In that moment of indecision, the tears fell, creating little creeks down his face, like the snow melting in the warm spring air.

Jan looked up at Pastor Enoch. The pastor smiled at him through watery eyes.

"I must always remind myself at times like this, Jesus cried too. And He was the finest example of a man we've ever known."

104

Jan smiled. A big smile. And he laughed. Pastor laughed too. They both sat thoughtfully for a few seconds. Pastor's words were a lot to take in.

"God has also taught me a way to deal with the negative feelings I sometimes get. Those verses I mentioned? Psalm 139:13-15, Exodus 4:11-12 and Ephesians 2:10. I wrote them out on a three by five card to remind myself that God designed me just as I am and He designed me for a purpose.

"Tell you what, Jan. Let me give you my card. I'll make another one."

"Are you sure?"

"Yes, I'm sure. By the way, have you read the story of Gideon yet, Jan?"

"No."

"You must read that, Jan. Judges 6 and 7."

With that, the pastor began to pick up his tools.

Chapter 12

The cold air slapped Jan in the face as he closed the church door behind him. The temperature had certainly dropped while he and Pastor Enoch had been talking. When the icy breeze seized his fingers, nose and ears, he stuffed his hands into his coat pockets, hugging his school books between his left arm and his side.

Ahead of him, about a block away, a couple of teenagers stood smoking along the right side of the road. Jan kept to the left side. Traffic on the side streets increased as people made their trek back home for supper. The last rays of the sun could just be seen toward the western edge of town. As it dropped off the edge of the horizon, it gave way to the blueness of night.

As he walked, he turned over the pastor's words in his head. The chill in the outside air had cooled off the enthusiasm for the pastor's words some. They had opened a whole other world of ideas though. If Pastor Enoch was right, the ideas changed a lot for Jan. Did other men really have fears too? All men? They didn't act like they did.

Jan's father never looked like he had ever been afraid of anything. Of course, there was still the high school principal's claim his dad had been a coward during the war. Jan knew traits could be passed down from parents to children. So, maybe that was true.

His mind felt locked in a struggle. Two sides, two theories. He wanted to believe Pastor more than anything. All men had fears. That would mean Jan really was a man, as the pastor had said. Yet, Mr. Sobear would argue otherwise. According to his view, there was just the weak and the strong. And it was always nature's choice that the strong should survive and flourish in this world.

"Evening, Reverend," came the voice of one of the smoking teenagers across the street.

Jan kept quiet and continued walking.

"Yeah, halleluiah," said the other with a snicker.

Jan ignored them. If that was all the mocking they would do, that wasn't bad. He considered himself lucky.

"Hey, wait," Jan suddenly heard one of them say. "That was Richards. The wimp."

With those words, Jan recognized the voice of Weasel Briler.

No, he thought. Not now.

His heart sunk. His soul curled up inside him again. He could hear the two sets of footsteps behind him getting closer. Picking up their pace. Five blocks still remained between him and his house. He could run, but his stomach had already begun to react. Weasel probably ran faster than him anyway. He probably wouldn't make it home fast enough.

"Richards," said Weasel, striking him hard on the shoulder hard as he came alongside him. It really hurt.

The other, older teenager snorted and bumped shoulders with Weasel.

"Saw you coming out of the church. You been praying?"

Jan remained silent. He concentrated on his shoes stepping firmly on the pavement.

"Whatcha praying for?"

"Maybe he was prayin' he wouldn't get beat up tonight," the older teenager said. It was Weasel's turn to bump his shoulder and snicker.

"You was praying for bigger muscles, weren't you?" asked Weasel.

Jan didn't answer.

Suddenly, Weasel's hand clamped itself around Jan's upper arm.

"Oops. It didn't work, Jannie." He turned to his older friend. "He ain't got no muscles."

"Maybe he ain't a man," said the other, placing his hand contemplatively on his chin.

He ain't. The negative voice joined in now.

"Are you a man, Jannie?"

Jan's stomach churned powerfully now. Bubbles seemed to pop throughout its contents. The sensations were getting bad. He couldn't tell which end it might spew out of if this situation continued.

"Are ya, Jannie? Come on. Show us."

You have nothing to show. You know it.

"Prove you're a man, Jannie. We want to see."

"Leave me alone." The words came out quietly but deep and gravelly.

"Ooo." Weasel raised his thick, black eyebrows. "We're finally getting a rise out of him."

"I think he really wants to show us," said the other.

"Come on, Jannie." The playfulness in Weasel's voice began to fade now. Intensity fell down from his eyelids and latched onto his pupils.

Jan felt his hands tighten into fists inside his coat pockets.

"You're not a sissy, are you, Jannie?"

Water gathered in his eyes. His fists trembled. And he could feel the acid in his stomach making its way up to his esophagus.

"Huh?" Weasel shouted.

Weasel's right hand shot out suddenly striking Jan solidly in the stomach. Jan lurched forward grabbing his belly. His school books dropped one at a time onto the pavement. Then, he felt the eruption from his stomach coming upward.

Again came Weasel's fist. This time it struck alongside Jan's nose. All at once, vomit shot from his mouth. Weasel leaped back in shock as half-digested food splattered upon the street. Jan fell onto his hands and knees. A second eruption followed. It spewed out between his hands and onto the front of his coat. Then, as if to add insult to injury, he felt warmness run down the bottom half of his face. Drops of crimson splattered on the pavement. Jan glanced up, wondering if he should expect another attack from Weasel.

The other teenager patted Weasel on the back as they stood together looking down upon him. Smirks formed on their faces.

Jan only felt weak, exhausted.

The other guy chuckled. "He couldn't even fight. He just got sick. What a sissy."

Weasel gave one of his biggest Bluto smiles. Then, they both turned, laughed, and walked on.

Sissy. The negative voice repeated the word in case Jan hadn't heard it the first time.

Jan fell back onto his butt and rested his back against the snowbank behind him. Vomit smeared the front of his coat. It also soaked the knees of his pants.

"Hey, Richards. Smile. God loves you," Weasel shouted back at him. They laughed.

Sissy, Sissy-boy. Again the words echoed in his head.

Jan grabbed a chunk of snow from the snowbank. He pressed it against his nose and laid his head back. Then, he swallowed. All his strength had left him. If he did have any muscles, they seemed to have given up.

All that remained of the sunset now was a bluish-green glow on the horizon, as it surrendered to dark skies. Everything became cloaked in darkness. As a couple of cars passed by him, he realized the shadows must have made him invisible within their shade.

He had to formulate a plan. Somehow he had to clean up before his mother saw him. If she saw him like this, she would call someone. Probably the sheriff. He couldn't let that happen. The sheriff had been a friend of his father's. What would he think if he saw Jan covered in vomit and unable to have thrown at least one punch at his attackers? What would he think?

Sissy. Sissy-boy. The negative voice answered him.

No. He couldn't allow that to happen. Imagine all the kids at school finding out. Even the readers wouldn't allow him to sit with them then. Everyone hated sissies.

Jan removed another chunk of snow from the snowbank and began to scrub green coat. If his coat and pant legs were damp when he got home, it would look like he had just fallen. That would be okay. The snow in his other hand should stop the nosebleed shortly. He could use the snow to wash the blood off his face as well.

Cleaning himself off, he picked up his books and started walking again. His stomach ached from both its upheaval and the slug to it. The acidy pit of his stomach would ache and then the punch site on his gut would throb as he stumbled down the street. When he was hurting, even a few blocks felt like miles. He kept shifting the school books from one hand to the other, giving each a break to warm in his coat pockets. The hand holding the books he pressed against his stomach in an attempt to control the pain.

He walked as upright as best as he could despite the discomfort. The only disadvantage was he was only able to take short steps without more pain. Jan had become used to getting around with stomach pain during one of his episodes. He had hidden his pain at school many times – especially when he would run out of excused absences. Feeling pain wasn't manly. Never let another guy know you're hurting.

Sissy, Sissy-boy. The negative voice continued to mock him.

Slowly, he made his way down Chestnut Street toward Bateau Avenue. Cars continued up and down the main thoroughfare at a pretty steady pace. It might not be easy to make it across. At least, not without attracting attention.

The weakness made him stop for a moment as he approached Bateau Avenue. His right arm hugged a large elm tree along the sidewalk and he leaned against it. He took short deep breaths as he relaxed. Long breaths made his stomach hurt more. Only one large white house stood between him and the corner. Not much farther after that. He just didn't want to stand at the corner, exposed, for very long.

Any of the cars traveling down Bateau might contain someone from school or even someone who knew his mom.

Unexpectedly, someone walked past the side of the white house facing Bateau and waited to cross at the same spot Jan wanted to. He carried a snow shovel in his hand. It was Steve. He must have been out shoveling some elderly people's driveways for extra cash.

Slowly, Jan released his arm from around the large tree. He pressed his shoulder more against the bark instead to steady himself. Then cautiously, he walked backward until he could no longer see Steve. If Steve saw him like this would he conclude Jan had had more than a sick stomach? His best friend proved to be more perceptive in situations than his mom did. Again his stomach began churning.

No. Not again. He was already weak enough. He didn't know what another bout of heaving would do. He envisioned himself crawling on his hands and knees, pushing his books along, to get the rest of the way home.

Of course, Jan could only blame himself. Normal guys never faced situations with bullies. Only sissies received this. Another reason Gunwale was no place for sissies. After graduation, he would have to leave.

That's when the next eruption hit. It spilled down onto the sidewalk. His shoulder slipped from the old elm tree. Down onto his knees, he fell again. The pain in his stomach reached a new, higher level. That seemed to make the bruised area from Weasel's punch ache more too.

Make it stop. Please, God, make it stop. Have mercy on me.

"Jan?" Steve's voice sounded like that of an angel standing over him. "Aw, man. Are you sick?"

Jan nodded, fearing speaking might trigger another eruption.

"You're going to be okay. I'll help you home."

Stepping around the vomit, Steve walked over behind him.

"Can I help you stand?"

Jan nodded.

Gently, Steve's hands came up under his armpits. Smoothly and slowly he raised Jan up off the ground. Then, steadying him with one arm, Steve reached down and also grabbed Jan's books from the snow. Softly, they took a small step forward and then another. Steve held him tightly, making taking steps easier.

As they came to the street corner, they barely stopped at all. Steve held up the hand carrying the snow shovel with Jan's books pressed against his side. Traffic stopped without complaint. Jan's body felt lighter to him. Steve must be taking on a lot of his weight too.

They passed Steve's house and he stopped briefly, tossing the shovel into the driveway. Resetting his hands to carry just the books now, Steve braced up Jan again. Slowly they made their trek to Jan's house about a block away.

Steve helped him up the steps and into the house. The kitchen sat dark and quiet. Jan's mother was out with some friends from work. She knew Jan would be working late with the reverend. Likewise, Sue would be over at a friend's house too.

Steve flipped the light switch. The pink kitchen leaped to life. A note from Jan's mom sat on the kitchen table. She explained there were TV dinners in the freezer.

"Didn't your mom cook you dinner?"

Steve's mom was always the perennial housewife and mother. She stayed home all day, cleaned and baked, like something out of an old TV show. However, she was also the mom who welcomed her children's friends from around the neighborhood and made them always feel at home.

"I'm okay. Don't feel much like eating anyway."

"Oh, yeah. I guess you wouldn't."

Steve helped Jan into a kitchen chair. Jan let out a deep breath as he dropped onto the seat.

"Thanks, Steve."

Steve looked down at his long-time friend.

"What happened to your nose?"

"Huh?"

"Looks like there is some blood crusted under it."

112

Jan quickly wiped the blood away with the side of a finger. "I must have hit my nose when I fell to the ground earlier."

Steve frowned. "Are you sure you are okay?"

"Yeah," Jan said looking away from him. "I just need to rest."

"Do you need help getting to the couch or your bed?"

"I think I'll be going to bed."

Again his friend helped him up. They walked together into his bedroom and Jan dropped down onto his bed.

"How long before your mom gets home?"

"Probably not long. I'll be okay. The bathroom is only a door away."

"Okay, pal. But if you need anything, let me know."

"Thanks again, Steve. I really appreciate it."

"No big deal."

"You seeing Jenny tonight?"

"No, she has a load of homework to do. I think I might call up Mindy though."

"Your folks will let you make a long-distance call?"

"Yeah. Gotta pay for it with my own money, though."

"One of these days, Jenny is gonna find out."

"Naw. I'm too good. Take care, Jan."

"Bye."

That evening, Jan lay on his side in his bed, his arms holding his gut gently and legs limp. Tears flowed from his eyes in steady streams. Words kept coming back into his head.

A boy has got to be tough.

He couldn't even fight. He just got sick.

Sissy-boy, You're just food.

The words kept replaying in his head. Mr. Sobear was right. He was just food for guys like Weasel and Mark Fury. Sobear had all science to back him up. Only the strong survive.

Jan's mind went back to the conversation his parents had years ago. Evidently, the Quarry boy got tired of being someone's food. He felt there was no other escape. Rather than let someone else choose his

113

downfall, he chose his own.

Gunwale is no place for sissies.

It seemed to be true. Most of the men in town seemed to have been on some sports team or they hunted. That's all guys talked about. Both activities took bravery. And that is what Jan had always lacked. Every time he tried to reach down inside himself to pull up some courage, there was nothing there. Why? Had nature chosen him to be weak?

Perhaps he too was destined for the Quarry boy's fate. Maybe that boy had the right idea. Why go on if all you were ever going to be in life was someone's food? The negative voice made Jan wonder the same thing. It would be horrible to live your life with a voice in your head constantly taunting you. Was "sleep in death" truly the answer? That did come from the Bible too.

The Bible. Jan shoved his hand into his pants pocket. He pulled out the three by five card Pastor had given him. Wiping tears from his eyes, he set it down on beside him on the bed. The card read:

God designed me

"For you formed my inward parts;

you knitted me together in my mother's womb.

I praise you, for I am fearfully and wonderfully made.

Wonderful are your works;

my soul knows it very well." (Psalm 139:13-14)

He even created the parts I don't like or understand their purpose

Then the Lord said to him, "Who has made man's mouth? Who makes him mute, or deaf, or seeing, or blind? Is it not I, the Lord? Now therefore go, and I will be with your mouth and teach you what you shall speak." (Exodus 4:11-12)

He designed me to fulfill a purpose in His greater plan.

For we are his workmanship, created in Christ Jesus for good works,

which God prepared beforehand,

that we should walk in them. (Ephesians 2:10)

And he wanted so much to believe Pastor Enoch. But that meant trusting in something without the slightest bit of evidence. Surrendering to what seemed impossible.

He was trying to remember what all Pastor Enoch had said. Something about fear every guy had. Men were always trying to prove they were men. They did not realize God had already made them men from the beginning. Or something like that. And somehow faith figured into breaking the need to prove yourself. Trusting God had made you as He meant you to be.

Jan hadn't been great at prayer. He did it with the family at mealtime and during crises sometimes. But Pastor Enoch often said in his sermons people need to pray more and read their bibles more. It was through such things, people grew closer to God.

Yet the negative voice prodded him with doubt.

How could a God love you? Remember the locker room. You look nothing like the other guys. You act like a sissy, afraid of everything. Everyone. Men are everything you are not.

Jan rolled over onto his back and stared up at the ceiling of his bedroom. The darkness of the room made the ceiling so thoroughly black, it seemed almost not to be there. It looked more like a portal into some other world.

"God, am I really becoming a man? I just don't know. Everything seems to point out that I'm nothing but a sissy. Mark says it. My dad … he said it too. Am I really a man? Pastor says I am because you made me to be one. But then, why do others reject me? Why don't I fit in? Why am I an outcast among other guys? What's wrong with me?"

Because you're a sissy. Sissy-boy. No one wants to be around a sissy.

Jan could feel the trickle of warm water down his cheeks again.

Only sissies cry. You are such a sissy.

His whole body shook. His left hand clutched the blanket beneath him and twisted it. His right hand rose, reaching toward the ceiling. Fingers sought for help.

"How do I break away from this curse? I just don't know. A guy can't be both a man and a sissy, can he? He's either one or the other. If people say you're a sissy, then you can't be a man. But, Pastor says You created me to be a man before I was born."

Sissy. You're no man. Even air is wasted on you.

Then, out of the darkness of his mind, a bible verse he'd heard came forward.

"Whoever wants to be my disciple must deny themselves and take up their cross and follow me." the other voice, the gentle one, reminded him.

"I'll follow you anywhere," Jan cried out. "But tell me what it means to be a man. Show me."

Silence sealed the room. Maybe Jan's mind too. The negative voice stopped. Not even a whisper now.

"God?"

Jan looked up expectantly at the dark expanse in the ceiling. His fist released the blanket from its grip and pushed it off the bed. Stillness and quiet could be felt. Peace. But no answer.

Jan dropped his right hand onto the bed. His mind felt relaxed now. In fact, a bank of exhaustion swept over his thoughts, clouding them. Muscles released their tenseness.

In the darkness, cool air blanketed his damp form. Sheets below him gently blotted the drops of perspiration from his back. One eye struggled to keep a vigil on the ceiling. Then, sleep kissed his forehead.

Chapter 13

Two days later, when the school bell rang for the weekend, Jan breathed deeply. The day was over at last! No need to dodge bullies. Both Mark Fury and the Weasel appeared to have lost interest in Jan for the time being. He hurried to his locker, grabbed his books, ran out the doors and took his place on the bus.

To his shock, Steve came in and plopped down next to him.

"Where's Jenny?"

"Her mom and dad picked her up from school. I guess the whole family is heading downstate for the weekend to see some relatives. They wanted to get an early start."

"So, are you free tonight?" Jan asked, hoping for something to look forward to.

"Looks like it."

"Cool. I'll be over after supper. I'll grab some goodies too."

"You want to sleep over? I don't have anything going on tomorrow as far as I know."

"Okay."

They walked back to Steve's place together. The snow had been melting a little and forming mud puddles along the streets. The snowbanks were now a muddy gray color from cars splashing through the puddles. The leafless trees added to the grayness of the day.

Leaving Steve at his house, Jan dropped off his books at home and wrote a quick note to his mom. She was going out with friends tonight anyway. He walked up to Roch's Party Store. He grabbed their favorite snacks and quickly paid for them. Then, he made his way back to Steve's house.

They ran up the stairs to Steve's bedroom immediately. As soon as the door shut, each grabbed a pop. Jan tore open the bag of chips. Steve graciously played his favorite album and the talk began. Topics flew by, but inevitably everything converged on Steve's last date with Jenny. A smile found its way back onto Jan's face. Music swam around them and mingled with the posters of girls, cars, and bands on Steve's walls.

A full bag of triangular-shaped cheese chips and both bottles of yellow pop in green bottles were consumed during the next few hours. This was what Jan wanted every night of adulthood to be like.

"I think Mindy is coming up next weekend," Steve said out of the blue.

"Oh, yeah?"

"And guess what? My grandparents will be gone for the weekend."

"Okay." Jan looked at Steve quizzically.

"Remember? I have the key to their house, so I can shovel their walkway."

Jan nodded, still not sure of where Steve was going.

"We're gonna do it, Jan. They have this guest bedroom and we're going to use that."

Jan wasn't sure what to say.

"I get to finally find out what being a man is like. Mindy and I planned it all out."

"Wow." Jan didn't know what to say. Pastor's word popped into his mind again. Men were always trying to prove they were men. They did not realize God had already made them men from the beginning.

"What about Jenny?" Jan asked.

"I've already come up with an excuse. Besides, I'm doing this for her."

"Huh?"

"To gain experience. All women want a guy who knows what he's doing. I figure by the time Jenny and I get around to it, I'll be an expert."

"Lights out!" came Mrs. Reddy's voice from the hall, just as Steve's alarm clock clicked off the eleventh hour. Mr. Reddy had probably fallen asleep in his recliner again. From that moment on, silence is what Steve's parents expected to hear. Steve and Jan stripped down to their briefs. As Jan climbed into the twin bed nearest him, Steve stood, stretching out briefly. It was easy to see why he always had at least two girlfriends. He had a broad chest with some hair on it and well-defined muscles. They weren't huge like The Phantom's, but large enough to get noticed in a t-shirt on any beach.

Steve, placing a finger to his lips, walked over to his stereo and plugged in his headset. He stretched out the cord between their two beds, placed the headset on the floor and adjusted the earmuffs so they were eschewed. Steve turned down the volume on the stereo and flipped off the light. Over the course of their friendship they had learned what levels of sound were acceptable so as not to alert parents they were secretly still awake whenever they held a sleep-over. It had become a field of expertise to them.

As they listened to the music, Jan still felt restless.

"Hey, Steve," he whispered.

"Yeah?"

"Are you still thinking of going into the army after you graduate?"

"Yup. I sure am. You can make a good start for yourself doing that. What do you think you'd like to do, Jan?"

"I don't know. The military definitely would not accept someone like me."

"Oh, yeah. 'Cause of that problem with your intestines."

"Yeah. It's under control again for now, but I never know when something might ...." Jan's voice began fading. He really didn't want to talk about his chronic illness again.

"Too bad for that. I really look forward to joining up. They have a good plan for getting guys a college education afterward, if they want one."

"Think you'll go to college, Steve?"

"I don't know. Jenny and I will probably get married once I've gotten settled on a base. The army itself can train me for most of what I want."

"What about Mindy?"

"She's okay to date, but I think Jenny and I are more compatible. Do you think you'll go to college, Jan?"

"I don't know. I'm not sure I have what it takes."

"You should go to one of those art schools. I bet you'd do really well at one of them."

"Maybe."

"Think you'll get married someday, Jan?"

"I'd like to."

"I wonder why some people never do."

"I don't think some people are cut out for it," Jan stated flatly.

"You mean like getting along with another person?"

"Yeah, kind of. But maybe some people aren't built for it."

"Built for it? What do you mean, Richards?"

"Well, some people never go out on dates because they know they will never be what other people expect them to be like, … you know, … physically."

"But different people have different ideas about the type of person they want to marry, Jan."

"Yeah, but it seems like there are certain things everybody seems to require in the opposite sex."

"Like what?"

"I don't know. Like my sister and her friends always talked about the kind of men they wanted to marry, and it seemed pretty much the same."

"People say lots of stupid things, Jan. I've said stuff like that myself. It is part of the game to make the other side jealous. The truth is, it really doesn't matter. Look at the girls and guys who date in our school. They don't all look like they came out of 'Teen Beat' magazine."

"You really think it is part of a game?"

"I'm positive."

"I'm not so sure, Steve."

"I am. So, what kind of guy did your sister's friends say they wanted?"

Jan quickly switched subjects and began talking about the music playing between them. Just thinking about the differences between his body and any other men's triggered emotions of failure and being unmasculine. When words about body differences were spoken, the words caused even more emotional pain. Seeing differences made him feel worthless.

* * * * *

The next morning, Jan plodded into Steve's family's bathroom. It was much larger than the one at his house. The sink area was much wider, with a big mirror taking up the whole area behind it. Jan's bathroom only contained a small mirror on the medicine cabinet above the sink.

He took off his clothes and let them flop onto the floor near the bathtub and shower unit. Slowly, he raised his head. There in the mirror appeared a teenager he hadn't noticed before. A teenager whose face he recognized but whose naked body seemed foreign and far more mature looking than he knew.

He stared at the image. When had all that happened? He looked down at himself and then back at the reflection. It was really him.

Somehow, through that small, fragile, awkward body, God was bringing forth a man. He wondered how that could be. Jan had been so sure nothing like that was in him. As he stared at the reflection, he thought he heard a new voice in his head. It was unlike the other voice. Not critical, but warm and gentle.

You are my man.

A shiver passed through Jan. His legs trembled. He felt like he was coming out of a dream. For an instant, he stood there with the reflection and the presence of the voice surrounding him. But there was no shame. A feeling of warm welcome hugged his soul. Then, the room reformed around him.

No sooner had the room come back, when the door opened and Steve stepped in. He looked over at Jan's unclothed form with no change of expression. Jan froze between wanting to cover himself and wanting to show he was proud of who he was becoming.

"This is no time to be admiring your hunky body, Richards. I got a sister waiting to get in here. She has dance practice."

Hunky body. Jan smiled at the fact Steve had used that term with him. Then, "You'll catch up," the words from the TV show came back to him.

Jan laughed as Steve grabbed a comb from the sink, wiggled his eyebrows, and made a quick exit. He climbed into the shower, looking back one more time at the mirror before closing the red, yellow and an orange flowered shower curtain. As he lathered up, his mind pondered the strange new image and the realization that Mark Fury's insults were not true. They hadn't been true for some time. Mark had gotten Jan to believe a lie. That changes everything, Jan thought. Everything.

* * * * *

On Monday morning, the new image of himself brightened his day. Yet, part of the experience still seemed like a dream. What was the word people used? Surreal. The truth of what he really looked like seemed too big to fit into his head. Yet, he couldn't deny what the mirror showed him. He was physically becoming a man. But sissies couldn't be real men, could they? Feelings of hope and excitement mixed with caution and confusion. And as he walked out the door of his house, he took a deep breath and then headed off to meet Steve at a quicker pace than usual.

In gym, he did what Mr. Guideron told him to do earlier in the semester. He followed Coach's instruction and did as he was asked, regardless of the outcome. Coach had told him and a couple other guys to go work out in the weight cage on the mezzanine. The two others were from the freshman class, so Jan didn't really know them. They talked back and forth as they went around to different stations. Jan just followed, staying a step behind them,

After a few minutes, one of them spoke up. "Hey, who's rappelling now?"

The two freshmen went over and leaned on the railing to watch. Once again, Jan followed. This was probably the most frightening aspect of Boy's Individualized Sports. Heights like that were not in Jan's comfort zone.

The coaches had constructed a platform way up near the ceiling of the gym on the north wall. Everyone in Boys Individual Sports was required to perform two tasks on the platform. First, a student must climb up the net attached to the platform, connect the rope to their harness and then walk down the side of the wall, holding on to the rope.

Second, the student was required to climb up the net again and rappel off the front of the platform. The rope carried the student underneath the platform where their feet bounced off the wall and they continued their downward descent to the mat on the floor. There, Coach held a belay line connected to the student's harness to keep them safe.

The wooden platform was built between two ceiling rafters, about six feet by nine feet and held in place by pipes beneath it as well. Two experienced students were stationed on the platform as spotters to watch each student's descent. Coach and Tim, the senior assistant, watched at the bottom for assist if needed. Today was Mark's turn to rappel.

"It's that Mark guy," said the freshman farthest from Jan.

"He acts pretty cool. I betcha he has no problems doing this," said the freshman next to Jan.

"Yeah, he's pretty manly. You see all the chest hairs he has?" responded the first freshman.

Mark rappelled down the gym wall as if he did it every day. No flaws, no problems, no apparent fear. Again he climbed up. The guys on the platform hooked him up to the rope.

Holding the rope with gloved hands, Mark backed up to the front of the platform. He glanced down to see Tim and Coach nod affirmatively. Stepping back, his feet pressed down onto a metal pipe running along the front of the platform. Slowly, he allowed some of the rope to slip through his fingers and he leaned backward.

"You're good," came Coach's voice.

Suddenly, Mark dropped down and his body swung under the platform. His tennis shoes tapped the wall. He bounced back out like a pro and dropped again. After the third bounce off the wall, he landed on the floor next to Coach and Tim with precision.

"Good job," Coach said.

Mark released the rope and detached his harness. It dropped to the floor. Picking it up, he began to strut off in his usual manner when suddenly something seemed to catch his foot. He toppled in a very awkward motion. His body made a loud splat sound as it hit the floor, which echoed throughout the big room. The whole gym burst out in laughter. Angry, Mark looked back and saw nothing. He glanced at his hand and saw he was still holding his own harness.

"Did someone leave their harness there?" Coach shouted, assuming Mark had tripped over one. "I keep telling you guys to put them in the milk crate where they belong, not leave them in the open for someone to trip over." Coach looked down, but there was no harness at Mark's feet. Nothing was on the floor.

Shaking his head, Coach reached out his hand to Mark, but he refused the gesture. Pulling himself up off the floor, Mark threw his equipment against the wall and walked over to the bleachers. Heavy breathes came from his red face. Coach gave him a glaring look.

A guy came walking up the stairs over to the railing where Jan and one of the other guys stood.

"What happened to him?" the new guy asked.

"He tripped over someone's equipment," said the guy nearest Jan.

"There wasn't any equipment on the floor around there."

"Maybe he tripped over his own harness then," said the other freshman.

Jan had been watching. He knew Mark had been carrying his own harness when he fell. He hadn't seen any other harness lying on the floor either. Their bright colors should have made it stand out against either the wooden floor or the dark green mats directly below the platform. Strange. What did Mark trip over?

When class was finished, Jan followed the others into the locker room. There was still some anxiety as he undressed. Mustering his courage, reminding himself God made him as he was, he walked toward the shower room. As he walked in, he heard some voices in the far corner. Barry Lancer talked with a couple of other guys in the far corner as they lathered up. It was at that very moment the image he saw in the mirror at Steve's house came back to mind.

The truth was there wasn't much difference at all between Jan and the other guys showering at the other end. They didn't all have hair on their chests either. Their hands were similar in size to Jan's rather than the great grizzly paws he remembered on his dad. Sure, they had bigger muscles, but they had spent their years in athletic pursuits. Jan was an artist. Art didn't require muscles. Everything else about them looked far more similar than they did different.

They were all men. It was as if Jan had been still seeing himself through the eyes of a middle schooler until that very moment in Steve's bathroom a couple of days ago.

Suddenly another figure came up and stood in front of the second showerhead to the right of Jan.

Mark Fury, his face in a scowl, began turning the shower knob. Water shot out into his face unexpectedly. He sputtered and shook it off with a grimace.

Jan caught a laugh before it escaped his mouth. The back of his hand came up and covered his amusement.

Mark saw the movement. He turned his head. "What?"

"I didn't say anything."

"Don't even think of it, Sissy-boy," Mark whispered in anger with a hissing voice.

But Jan couldn't help but smile. First Mark's accident in the gym, being laughed at and now being smacked in the face by water. This was not Mark's day.

"And get that smile off your face before I shove it down your throat."

Jan shut the water off and looked over at Mark who glared at him. The bully stood there, resting on the balls of his feet, with his chest, puffed out and his hands tightened into fists. Water dripped off his face and rolled down his body. Truthfully, he wasn't all that impressive. He had less muscles than Barry and most of the other athletes in the class.

Jan could still see differences between Mark and himself, but those parts of Mark which looked so impressive before now looked ludicrous on him as he stood there dripping wet, with a slight shiver, trying to seem tough. There were differences between Mark and the other guys too. Strangely, Mark's most outstanding difference now was all the scars on his body. Mark tilted his head slightly and drew up his fist, leaning toward Jan. His eyes narrowed. Jan smiled and grabbed his towel.

"We're settling this after school," he said in a low voice. Immediately, water trickled from his hair into his eyes and he had to wipe them. He looked like a puppy coming out of the rain.

"Mark, you're a liar. I don't believe you anymore."

Confusion descended on Mark's face, sending the angry look down to the wet floor at their feet.

Turning on his heel, Jan walked off without looking back. Mark fumingly snorted in response.

"Hey, Mark. Nice trip you took today," said Barry laughing, as he and his friends followed Jan out of the shower room.

Jan walked over to his gym locker. He glanced down briefly below the towel. His legs seemed longer now than they used to and he could see muscle development there. It was probably from all the hiking he did on the trails behind the elementary school when no snow covered the ground. Why did he not notice the change earlier? His body did not have to mirror Mark's.

No doubt he had been indeed been born a boy and now God was bringing out the man He had already placed there. Jan lifted his head up slowly and glanced around the room. Guys talked and dressed themselves. Tall, short, thin, fat, lots of different body types. Some guys had muscular chests; others had flat, undefined chests; others' chests had more padding underneath. Some guys had hair all over their bodies; others had hair which was light and barely noticeable. There were guys who looked like they had just one long eyebrow instead of two. And everybody part came in a different size or appearance on some guy in the room.

Jan's body mirrored lots of other guys in different places. Tall, short, thin, fat, lots of different body types. Minor differences – that's what they all had. Somehow, there was a oneness to this group of people he hadn't felt before. They were the same.

As Jan opened his locker door, Pastor Enoch's words returned to his mind. "We try to keep up this facade that we are invulnerable. Deep inside, though, we are all hurting and searching for what will make us feel like men."

Were they all searching for what made them feel like men? Is that why some chose to play sports, others went hunting, and so on? Isn't that what he felt when he read the Phantom or Dick Tracy?

As he changed his clothes, Jan heard Mark cuss from the shower room. Something else must have gone wrong. Barry and some of the other guys chuckled. This time he didn't though.

Underneath the toughness, was Mark hurting also? Was fighting Mark's way of proving to himself he was a man? It seemed impossible, but it made sense.

Chapter 14

Jan returned home to find a note on the kitchen table from Sue saying she was eating at Heidi's house that night. No surprise there. He walked through the living room and into his bedroom, tossing his books on his desk.

Then he laid down on the bed. On his back. Visions from the previous days sprang into his mind. A smile came to his face. Had all that really happened? He felt differently about himself now – as if overnight he had become a real teenager. The proof was there. He was sure now.

And that other voice he heard in his head in Steve's bathroom. "You are my man," it said. It wasn't the negative voice. It wasn't Jan's thoughts either. Pastor had said that God usually speaks to us today through the Scriptures. Usually. That was the word he used. Not always, but usually.

Then there were the events earlier in the day. Mark tripping. The realization neither Mark nor the other guys were way ahead of him in maturity. Telling Mark he was a liar. Where had the confidence to say that even come from? He was sure Pastor would say that came from God also.

Last week I prayed to God to show me who I was, Jan remembered. I thought He would answer me that night, but He didn't. Yet, in the last few days, my questions have been answered.

"It was You, wasn't it?" he whispered looking up at the ceiling. "You answered my prayers. You told me who I was." Suddenly, Jan remembered some other words Pastor had said during a sermon: that God worked on His own timetable, not on ours.

Jan took the new energy he felt inside, jumped up, and walked over toward his desk. His hip bumped his dresser as he walked in that direction. Suddenly, he heard the baseball roll round in his sock drawer again. He opened the drawer, picked up the ball, and held it in his hand. A feeling of responsibility came upon him. He would have to do something with this soon. When he was younger, he had thought of throwing it away or burning it somewhere. Something always held him back. After what had recently happened to him, he would soon have to do something with that. It didn't belong there. He set the ball back in the drawer and closed it.

Walking away, he went behind his desk and pulled out his chair. He sat down and opened his school books and looked over his homework. He could probably finish it before his mom came home.

In fact, that turned out to be true. His mom arrived just as he closed his last school book. He heard the door open and shut. Then came his mom's voice.

"Jan?"

"Yeah," Jan replied as he stepped out into the kitchen.

"Are you feeling okay? You forgot to bring the newspaper in." She flopped the folded paper down onto the kitchen table.

"Sorry. Thinking about other things, I guess."

"I was thinking about hot dogs and macaroni and cheese for supper. What do you think?"

"Sounds good." Immediately Jan began to set the table with patterned plates decorated in dark blue designs, many representing farm life. The dark blue stood out boldly against the pink walls of the kitchen.

"So, how was your day, Mom?"

She stared over at him as she drew a cigarette out of her purse. "Are you sure you're feeling okay?"

"I'm fine. But I do have a question I've been wanting to ask you."

"What's that?" she said lighting the cigarette.

"Mom, I overheard the principal say something about Dad the other day."

"Oh?" she looked a little apprehensive and took a long drag on her cigarette.

"It was about D-Day."

She released a huge cloud of smoke. "Oh. That old story."

Old story?

"Way before you were born, when we were still in high school, your dad dated another girl here."

"Mrs. Fury?"

"He mentioned her, too? It figures. His car is over at her place enough. Yeah, she had her hooks in your dad back then. He was an ambitious, hardworking man, of course, as he always had been. She thought he could take her places.

Jan's mom filled a pot with water and poured the macaroni noodles into it, placing it on the stove.

"There was one night, over at Dad Hancock's Soda Shop, I was there relaxing with some other girls. Your dad came in and plopped down. I could tell something was bothering him as he sat down a couple booths away. He just kept staring at the tabletop. I knew he was going with Eleanor, Mrs. Fury, but she was nowhere around. Your dad looked like he had lost every friend in the world.

"So, I excused myself and went over and sat across from him. I knew him a little from classes but we hadn't talked much because he belonged to Eleanor. Well, after a few minutes of chit-chat, he told me they had broken up. Your dad wanted to join the army and go off and fight in the war. She didn't want him to go. She was afraid he'd die over there and it would ruin her plans. Of course, your dad was stubborn and always protective of others. He felt it was his duty."

Mom dug three hot dogs out of a package. "You want two, right?'

"Yes, please."

The hot dogs plopped into a second pot on the stove. Turning up the burner on the stove, she took another drag off her cigarette and crossed her arms. "Your dad and I dated a few times afterward. That made Eleanor furious. He went off to war but we kept in contact through letters. Eleanor decided to start her own war with me."

"Her own war?" Jan asked.

"That's what I called it, Jan. World War Eleanor. She'd send me nasty notes, spread rumors about me. Sometimes write on my locker. Bump into me and make me drop my lunch. All kinds of things. She was downright vicious."

"Sounds like she was bullying you."

"'Bullying'? I never thought of it that way. We always used the word bullying for things happening in grade school. She was mean."

"Did you report her?"

"Once. But, you see, her father was the president of the bank. He donated a lot to the school. So, the principal overlooked it. I just kept avoiding her from then on."

"So, what about Dad and D-Day?"

"That day changed your dad forever, Jan. His platoon arrived at the beach in Normandy, but your dad became sick. Came down with the stomach flu or something while they were stationed in England. A medic ordered him to stay behind. The rest of his platoon died that day. Your dad felt tremendous guilt afterward. He felt like a coward."

"But he couldn't help that."

"I know. But it happened to a lot of soldiers. They call it survivor's guilt. He came back from the war feeling defeated. Feeling like he had let everyone down."

"He shouldn't have."

"Did you know he brought back medals from the war for saving the lives of other soldiers? He was honorably discharged. The papers are all in a dresser drawer somewhere. He may have felt like a coward for what happened, but that wasn't the way I felt. I always believed your dad surviving that day was a gift from God. It was as if God was saving him for me."

"What happened then?"

"When Eleanor figured out she'd never get your dad back, she came up with this lie that had bits of truth in it. She learned your dad's older brother broke down mentally during a battle and was sent back home disabled. Then, he ran off somewhere and we never saw him after that. Eleanor also learned not all the soldiers on D-Day were brave. Some ran off and hid until the tide turned. So, she concocted this story about your dad being a coward to hurt him."

"Did people believe her?"

"Unfortunately, yes. Her father, never doubting Eleanor's story, helped spread that rumor too. He held such a position of power as bank president, a lot of people believed."

"What did Dad do?"

"Nothing. He felt so bad about surviving, he began to wonder if they weren't telling the truth and his memories might be a lie."

"But Dad would never do that."

"No, Jan, he wouldn't. Your father was a very brave and trustworthy man. Instead, he devoted himself to his work. A little too much, I think. It was as if, somehow, he had to prove himself. To prove … something. I don't know. He lived with that shadow over him for the rest of his life."

"So, then Mrs. Fury married someone else, right?"

"That is a story in itself. She started dating this guy after Sue was born. She ended up getting pregnant before I was pregnant for you. There was what we called a 'shotgun wedding.' Her new husband didn't stick around though. He took off and she raised Mark by herself."

"Do you think she is still angry about Dad?"

"Last I knew, she still blamed him and me for all the failures in her life since. There's been a few times I've heard her say, when she was drunk, she wished she'd never met Mark's father. She wishes she'd married your dad instead. And Mark was standing right there next to her. I can't imagine what that has done to him."

"I imagine that hurt a lot." Jan stared at the carpeted floor.

"But, Jan, your dad loved you. You were his pride and joy."

"Are you sure?"

The question seemed to catch her off guard. She frowned and looked away for a moment, as if searching for her memory.

"Oh, yes, honey. I thought I told you. He never stopped talking about you around other people. And he loved your artwork. He wasn't an art person. He didn't know how to talk about it with you."

Water glinted at the bottom of her eyes. She looked deep into his eyes with a sorrowful look. Impulsively, she grabbed ahold of him and drew him close to her. Jan felt the water well up in his eyes also and immediately overflow down his cheeks. Not sissy tears though. These felt different, yet kind of the same. These were about love. He tightened his grip around his mother.

Around the supper table, Mom continued talking, telling him about their first dates, the letters she received from him during the war and the early days of their marriage. When they finished washing the dishes, they sat down and read the newspaper together.

Once he had caught up with the comics, Jan excused himself. "I have something I want to work on for Pastor Enoch."

"Can you turn the TV on for me, before you go? Channel nine."

Walking over to the TV, he turned it on and adjusted the channel tuner. Then he made his way into his room and plopped down on his bed. He reached over to his nightstand and grabbed his Bible sitting next to the three by five card Pastor had given him. Flipping the pages, he found Judges 6 and 7. The account told how the Israelite's land had been taken over by Midianites. Gideon was in hiding, grinding wheat to make bread. An angel appeared to him.

"The Lord is with you, mighty warrior," said the angel. The Lord then told Gideon to go and save Israel from the Midianites.

Gideon protested saying, "My clan is the weakest in Manasseh and I am the least in my family."

"I will be with you," God answered him.

Gideon was afraid and thought he might just be imagining this. So, God spent some time performing miracles to prove to Gideon He was indeed talking to him. Finally, Gideon gathered a small army of men. The night before they are about to attack the enemy's camp, God spoke to Gideon again.

"That same night the Lord said to him, 'Arise, go down against the camp, for I have given it into your hand. But if you are afraid to go down, go down to the camp with Purah your servant. And you shall hear what they say, and afterward, your hands shall be strengthened to go down against the camp.'"

Gideon did just that.

Jan had to reread the last verse. After all the miracles God had shone Gideon, he was still afraid. God didn't punish him for his fear. God actually allowed him to take his servant with him. He allowed him to be afraid.

Even better, God told Gideon and his group of 300 men all they had to do was blow some trumpets, break some jars and hold up torches from their positions around the enemy camp which held thousands of soldiers. God caused their enemies to turn on each other in the excitement. Gideon never even had to fight. He was called to war but never raised his fist.

God doesn't get mad just because you're afraid?

Now, Jan's mind went whirling again at the thought. It meant God wasn't the God Jan thought he knew. He laid back onto his bed, his eyes unable to focus on any particular objection in his room. He stared at the ceiling again.

Is this what Pastor meant when he talked about sessions with God? God talked to Gideon in the Bible, but He was also talking with me just now while I was reading that. So, He's telling me it doesn't matter that I have fears. This was another answer to my prayer, right?

Jan thought back to a few nights before. That night I prayed to God and asked Him to show me what it meant to be a man. And how He saw me. Is this His answer? You can be afraid and still be a man. He let Gideon do it. He didn't call Gideon a sissy.

Once again, his mind filled with recent memories. His prayer to God. The image in the mirror in Steve's bathroom. Mark's bad day. Dealing with Mark's insults. It was either a ridiculous string of coincidences or spiritual workings behind the scenes. So, was this how that growing faith Pastor mentioned begins?

Pastor Enoch had said, "It's all the same trust, Jan .... It all starts with the first step of faith."

"I want to put all my trust in You," Jan whispered, looking upward again. "Help me to trust in You more."

* * * * *

When Jan awoke the next morning, he was still in his clothes from the previous day. All he could remember was sorting through what all these revelations meant to him. Somehow, he had fallen asleep thinking about that. He sat up to what felt like a whole new world.

Part of his mind still wanted to doubt it could all be true. He had believed in the lies about himself for so long, it was hard to let them go. Yet, these revelations proved those beliefs to be false. He wondered what else was not as he imagined it to be.

Chapter 15

The next day as he arrived home after school, Jan heard Sue and her friend Melissa talking back in her bedroom. They were talking about the Summer Olympics coming up. They talked about how they wanted to see Olga Corbit perform gymnastics again. Although Olga came from Russia, she had become popular among women in America as a champion gymnast at the last Olympics in '72.

"I wonder if she will do well again this year?" Melissa asked.

"I think so. I mean, what else could happen? Some unknown little girl marches into the gym and dances away with the medals? I don't think so."

"I wonder if women will ever compete against men."

"I think so. Eventually. Look, we now know all the differences between men and women are just cultural. We teach boys to play with toy cars and girls to play with baby dolls. Women are always being held back in physical activity."

"Yeah, I guess that's true."

"Ms. Appenij says she believes the reason women lag behind men in physical competition is low self-esteem. If boys and girls were raised the same way, girls would have more confidence and be able to win in a competition against men. They just doubt themselves too much, that's all."

"Tell me about it. Men's lives are way too easy."

At that, Jan walked away into his own room. He plopped down on his bed and relaxed. He wasn't so sure anyone had an easy life. Being around his mom and Sue, he knew women's lives were not easy. And he was definitely glad God made him a guy.

Jan met with Pastor Enoch again on Wednesday. They had begun actually building the shelving unit. Pastor was letting Jan put screws in himself. He told Pastor he had read through Judges 6 and 7.

"What did you think of it?" Pastor asked.

"God didn't get mad because Gideon was afraid."

"That's right."

"But, what about all of the times God told men to be brave?"

"They needed to hear that. He was encouraging them. All those men who God spoke to were afraid. They weren't going to be able to do what He asked them by themselves. And the only way to be brave enough to do what God wanted was if they put all their trust in Him.

"Bravery doesn't come naturally to men because of our sinful nature. We act as if it does, but it doesn't. Bravery has to be taught. We must learn it. And the only way to be absolutely brave is to trust in God. That is why God puts us through trials in this life. We want to trust in ourselves, our own abilities. God wants the opposite. He wants us to trust in Him. The challenges we Christians face are simply ways God is trying to get us to trust Him more."

"Did God ever tell women to be brave?"

"That's a good question. Let's see. His angel told Mary not to be afraid. That's about the same as being brave. The judge Deborah in the Old Testament led an army of men into battle when the man God told to lead them, Barak, was too scared. And of course, Esther. She put her own life on the line to save others by appearing before King Ahauerus. Those are all examples of bravery. And no less bravery than any man."

"So, do you think God created guys and girls to be different? I mean, besides just body parts."

"What do you mean by different?"

"Well, to hear some people talk, women are inferior to men. Others say the only difference is in the way they are raised."

"Both are wrong. As we talked before, boys were meant to be boys and girls, as God designed them to be. There tends to be some general characteristics for each sex. Women tend to be more compassionate. Men tend to be the protectors of the family. However, there are lots of activities both are able to do. And remember, God created Adam and Eve separately. Adam needed Eve. He couldn't get along without her. So, how can she possibly be inferior?

"God also gives different instructions to men and women sometimes. He tells men, in several verses in the Bible, to treat their wives with gentleness, kindness, and understanding. The words he uses in the original language means to treat something as of great value, but also fragile. That leaves no room for abusive behavior toward women. Then, He tells women to respect their husbands. There is a difference."

"What about sports?"

"Sports are neither masculine nor feminine, Jan. I can't think of many activities which are. Sometimes God designs some people to go against the grain. That is, some may be given abilities we tend to associate with the opposite sex. He needs to have some of his followers be able to reach those who the average man or woman could not reach with the Gospel message. All Christians have a purpose in God's plan."

"So, if a guy is afraid of stuff, that doesn't mean he's more girl than guy?" Jan asked.

"Absolutely not, Jan. Remember, bravery is learned. God asks all believers to be brave at some point in their lives. Because that's where faith is born and grows.

"One of the things my generation has failed to do is appreciate those who God chose to be different. Instead, we have tended to act as if they are diseased. We have added our own qualifications to God's. We have made rules that men and women are supposed to be certain ways which are not based on Scripture at all. Some even twist Scripture around. That is why we must read God's Word for ourselves and not go by what is popular in today's society.

138

"Were there added rules for girls and guys when you were my age?" Jan asked.

"Oh, yes. Boys were called sissies if they enjoyed cooking, or like to sing in the choir, or almost anything to do with arts. Anything creative seemed to be considered feminine. And they were teased about it. Likewise, girls who were tomboys were looked down upon."

"It sure hasn't changed much."

"This problem of adding human rules to God's rules is nothing new. Mankind has always added its own rules to God's. In Jesus' time, they added rules to the Sabbath Day. When Jesus healed on the Sabbath, He broke their rules. Not God's rules. His teachings about God went against their self-created beliefs. They hated Him for it. We do better to follow God and His plan, as Jesus did.

"I think the church has a responsibility too. We need to take those who are different and help them to see themselves through God's eyes. We must help them reach the potential God gave them by recognizing who they are in Christ and guiding them through God's teachings. Too often we have failed them. And our enemy welcomes everyone."

* * * * *

The month of April came paddling into Gunwale bringing temperatures into the 50s in tow, banishing the remainder of snow on the ground. A lot of people took their canoes out of their garages and made sure their paddles and other equipment were together. A few hardy teens and adults actually began paddling up and down the AuSable to train for the upcoming canoe race the summer would bring to Gunwale.

Meanwhile, Jan finished his drawing of David and Goliath for Pastor Enoch. The pastor had it framed and hung on his wall in his office facing his desk. Together they finished the bookshelves. Pastor mentioned both during announcements before the worship service one Sunday. Several people actually congratulated Jan on his work.

Jan had begun taking his new art journal to school now. When teachers allowed for free time, he'd make use of it. Somehow, this new vision of himself made him feel even better about his artwork. No longer was he just drawing comic strip characters either, although he still enjoyed drawing them. Sometimes, he'd draw what he could see out the window; other times, classmate's faces when they weren't looking.

Meanwhile, Steve's evening of passion with Mindy a couple of weeks ago didn't go quite as he had expected. His grandparents came home early, and he had to come up with a lie to explain why the two of them were in the house alone together.

Mark caused no more trouble for Jan during that time. It was as if Mr. Guideron's warning and the embarrassing experience Mark had in gym had sucked out all the air from his puffed-up image. There were times Mark still gave Jan one of his glares, however, and he could feel Mark was only taking a breather from bullying activities. So, Jan reminded himself to put his faith in God daily to get him through. He also read the three by five card each morning too.

The warm temperatures had also opened up the trails behind the elementary school which ran along the river. It would be another month before buds sprouted to proclaim leaves were coming. The pines and cedars, however, waved their branches in the warm breeze as Jan walked along the trails once again, carrying his art journal. It felt good to be able to leave his bedroom. The forest meant freedom.

Fallen orange pine needles crunch beneath his tennis shoes as he walked along the pathway. Jan made his way along through the tall white and red pines. Their tall stances created a cathedral-like effect when he looked upward. It seemed as if nature itself were praising God. Jan didn't know if he would have looked at the forest this way a few weeks earlier. Now, everything appeared new and more alive. The new image he had been given of himself made him look at everything differently. More positively.

Holding on to his art journal tightly, he walked around the curving trail with determination. As he passed some fallen cedar trees lying partially in the river, he knew his destination wasn't much farther.

There lay a drainage pipe up ahead which ended in a cement slab running down into the river. In the river where the cement ended, reeds grew up. A dark green, they felt almost rubbery on the outside. The reeds always reminded Jan of those jungle movies where some guy was being chased and he hid in the reeds, using a carved out one as a breathing tube, to avoid capture.

As he approached the drainage pipe this time, he heard voices. His feet slowed down. The curve of the trail and pine trees prevented him from seeing who was there. One was a child's voice, but other sounded older and familiar.

"Empty out your pockets," said the older voice.

"Why?" the young boy sniffled.

"Because I said so. And you don't want to be hurt."

Slowly, Jan stepped quietly forward, peeking around trees. His dad had taught him how to step quietly when hunting, so as not to alert the animals. It was one of the activities Jan prided himself on. He might not be able to bring himself to shoot animals, but he could sneak up on them.

Finally, the people behind the voices came into view. The blond-haired boy in the green spring jacket appeared to be no more than ten. And the bully was Weasel Briler. Jan's first instinct was to sneak away from there. Then on the second thought, Pastor had said men were meant to be protectors. God created them that way.

What do I do? Jan wondered.

"You got some good candy there. Give it to me," Briler ordered the boy.

I can't think of anything else … except stepping out and confronting him, Jan thought.

He beat you up the last time you ran into him.

I know, Jan answered the negative voice. Weasel might laugh. He might bully me too. But that boy could turn out like I was – afraid of everything and everyone. I'd have wanted someone to stick up for me when I was his age, wouldn't I?

"Empty your other pocket."

"It's my lunch money," said the boy in a strained voice.

"Give it to me, sissy."

Sissy. Sissy-boy. The negative voice returned.

But this time, his soul didn't cower. It stood firm.

You are my man.

"Bravery must be learned." He remembered Pastor's words again.

"God be with me," Jan whispered. He set his art journal down on a nearby tree stump. Suddenly and with great forcefulness, Jan shouted, "What are you doing to that kid?!"

For the first time, Weasel jumped and stared in terror at the voice behind the tree. Jan tightened both his fists and stepped out into view. The next look on Weasel's face appeared a mixture of terror and confusion.

"Drop his stuff and get out of here!"

Jan slowly walked up to Weasel, continuing to keep his fists clinched. Weasel stood his ground, staring back at Jan. Though he tried to look angry, something was missing from Weasel's stare. The look of toughness on his face didn't seem 100 percent.

"I said, drop his stuff and leave," Jan repeated, staring straight into Weasel's eyes.

A questioning look came over Weasel's face. He seemed to be wondering just who this new Jan Richards was.

"No," Weasel said, but lacking his usual conviction.

"Yes, now," Jan said forcefully. And at that instant, Jan threw his chest forward. His arms shot out in front of him and his palms struck Weasel's shoulders. The bully's legs seemed to buckle in response. Weasel collapsed awkwardly onto the grass with a thud. There he lay, staring up at Jan, no more anger in his eyes. Only fear. To Jan's astonishment, Weasel wiped the candy from his sweaty palm, jumped up and ran off. Jan breathed out the air stored in his chest for those few seconds.

He ran away from me, Jan thought. He even gave up the little boy's candy. For all his tough-acting behavior, Weasel fled in fear when confronted. His toughness had been all a façade. And he claimed

Jan had been a sissy.

Jan glanced down when he caught movement out of the corner of his eye. The little boy bent over and began picking up his candy. Jan bent down too to help him.

Looking into the boy's eyes Jan said, "Are you okay?"

"Yeah. Did you see how fast he booked it out of here? Wow. Thanks."

"Do you still have all your money?"

"Yeah."

"Good. Do you live around here?"

"I live out by Kneff Lake, but my mom's a teacher here. I was waiting for her to finish getting ready to go home."

"Okay. Then, let's go back to the school. We'll report what happened to the principal."

"But I don't know who that other kid was."

"I do. We'll report it together," said Jan determinedly. "That way it won't be just your word against his."

"Cool." The boy smiled broadly.

Jan walked back and grabbed his art journal. Together he and the boy turned and climbed some wooden steps leading to the elementary school playground.

"Boy, that other kid sure was scared of you," the boy said looking up to Jan.

Jan looked up to heaven and smiled. Thank you, he said in his head.

* * * * *

After their explanation to the elementary school principal, the high school principal was called. The trails behind the school were still part of school property. Attempting to steal another student's money ranked high on the principal's list of serious offenses. This time the ole Weasel had gotten his paw stuck in an animal trap and the trapper was coming for him.

As Jan left the school and began his walk down Bateau Avenue, he heard someone call to him from down the street, closer toward his house.

"Jan! Jan!" the figure called as he came running. It was Steve, running as if someone was chasing him. There hadn't been many times in recent history Jan could recall Steve running to him.

"What's up?" Jan asked as his best friend came within about 20 feet of him.

"I gotta talk to you. Just got a call from Mindy. She's late."

"Late for what?"

"No. She thinks she is pregnant."

Jan's eyes and mouth dropped wide open. "But, I thought …."

"When my grandparents came home, we were just getting dressed."

"What are you going to do?"

"I don't know. Man, Jan, this ruins everything."

Jan thought back to their conversation at the sleepover a few weeks back. The plan had been to marry Jenny and go into the army. Jan wondered if the army would even take him after this.

"What are you going to do?"

"I don't know. You're the only person who knows besides Mindy and me," Steve said, worry and confusion pulling down his face and widening his eyes.

"And what about Jenny?"

"I don't know. This wasn't supposed to happen. I heard a girl couldn't get pregnant the first time." Steve sighed in disbelief. He looked like a little boy with a fake mustache now. Fear took possession of his whole face.

"Wow." It was the only word Jan could think of.

Steve was about to become a father. And despite his early maturity and seemingly tough demeanor, Steve looked terrified.

Neither his thick mustache nor the hairs on his chest peeking through his partially unbuttoned shirt could hide this moment. Scared and helpless – everything guys were told they must not be. It looked as

Afraid We Are Not
if even Steve would have to learn bravery now.

Chapter 16

The following Tuesday, after gym class, Jan sat on the boys' locker room bench listening to the others talk. He stretched his socks over his feet as Mark Fury passed by, bumping into him. His pant leg caught on Jan's art journal sending it onto the floor. It fell open to a sketch of Brenda Starr.

"What's this?" Mark said, picking up the notebook and looking at the drawing of Brenda Starr.

"Richards must read girls' comics. Brenda Starr."

"Mark, shut up," said Barry, combing his wavy, sandy hair. "My dad reads Brenda Starr too."

"Yeah. Her boyfriend with the eye patch is quite a tough guy too," added Eric Wolf, the blond-haired, tallest one of the group.

"That's some pretty good drawing, Jan," said Rocky Lyon, a teen with black hair and glasses, as he buttoned his shirt.

Mark dropped the notebook back on to the bench and walked out the door.

"That guy is such a jerk," Jan heard Andrew Rotterdam, a guy with a big afro hairstyle, say.

"You guys ever notice something?" Barry suddenly asked. "Fury is always bragging about being in fights and showing us his scars, but we never see anyone else come into the school that's been in a fight the same day. And he never tells us who he fought with. Who's he fighting, little kids?"

"He's never wanted to fight with me," said Rocky. "And he wouldn't be bragging if he ever did."

"Where does he live? Maybe he lives way out of town and fights guys from another county," Eric commented, as he shook his blond hair inside a towel.

"No, he lives just down the street from me," added Jan. "In town."

"You ever see him in a fight, Jan?" Barry asked.

"No. Never."

"I think he's lying," Barry said. "He's making it all up."

"So, where is he getting the scars from?" asked Andrew.

* * * * *

When Jan arrived home, he went straight to his bedroom as usual. On his bed, he pondered the locker room discussion. It reminded him of the current story in the comic strip, "Dondi." Dondi, the war orphan was brought to America by army soldiers to be adopted by the Wills family, his dad had once explained to him. Now Dondi had this group of friends called the Explorers Club who he had adventures with.

In the current story, Dondi met up with a new kid at his school called Timmy Slagg. He was an angry boy who came to school with black eyes and broken arms. Dondi thought Timmy wanted to fight him after he threw a rock at Dondi's dog. When Dondi went to Timmy's house, however, he inadvertently saw Timmy's mom beating him.

Between that comic and the talk in the locker room today, Jan's mind wouldn't let go of a memory it seized from years ago. When Jan and Mark Fury first met they began as friends back in early elementary school. That did not last long, however.

Jan had known Mark almost as long as he knew Steve. At first, they played together. Then, Mark found out that Jan didn't know much about playing sports. So, he tried to teach Jan about baseball. He kept getting frustrated when Jan took so long to learn each step of the process.

"Keep your eye on the ball," he would say as he pitched the ball to Jan.

Jan tried to watch the ball. Actually, that was the easy part. It was trying to hit the ball that was difficult. It seemed like he should be watching the bat more than the ball, so he could hit it. Jan just kept spinning around with the bat, swinging at air.

"Come on! What are you waiting for, Jan?" he started shouting very loudly.

Then, came another voice. It was Mark's mom. She called him inside.

Mark stayed inside for a few minutes. Jan could hear Mark's mom yelling at him, but couldn't tell exactly what she was saying. Jan wondered if he should go back home. Maybe he was in trouble too. He just couldn't tell what Mark's mom was so angry about.

Suddenly, Mark came out. His frowning face was red except his left cheek appeared to be more of a purple color. His eyes were narrow, too. Jan had never seen such a look on his face before.

"Can you still play?" Jan asked in a quiet voice from several feet away.

"Why couldn't you just hit the ball?" Mark said in an angry, low voice.

"I'm sorry. I don't know."

"You're a boy! You're supposed to know!" Mark's voice remained just above a whisper but thick with anger.

"I'm sorry," Jan repeated, unsure of what else to say.

"You sound like a girl! You swing like a girl too!"

And in an instant, Mark grabbed his baseball off the ground and hurled it at Jan. Quickly, Jan's arm went up to protect himself. He felt the hardball strike the side of his wrist. His eyes closed tightly, and he clenched his teeth together. He stopped any sound from coming out of his mouth, but two drops of water ran down his face. His hands went down, and he grabbed his right wrist to squeeze out the pain.

That was when Mark saw Jan's face. The two drops. The redness and narrow eyes remained set on Mark's face, but the corners of his mouth began to curl upward. The new look became even more frightening than the previous one.

"You're a sissy." The moment he spoke the words, Jan's mind seemed to take a photograph and store it away in an album deep inside. The only other thing Jan could remember after that was grabbing Mark's baseball and running home with it.

The next day, Jan saw Mark talking with some of the other boys at recess. The other boys smiled, looked over at Jan and began laughing. Making friends had never been easy for Jan, but from that day forward it seemed to become impossible. Who would want to become friends with a sissy?

That one incident became the beginning of years of bullying. Mark used the sissy nickname to hold power over Jan. Jan had nearly forgotten about Mark's mom's place in the story. Now, it all began to make sense. Mark must be his mother's scapegoat and he made Jan his.

So, Mark was lugging around this big secret and hiding it behind these stories about fighting other guys thought Jan. As tough as Mark pretended to be, he was really a kid being abused. Mark lived his whole life as a lie. Weasel too. Come to think of it, even Steve wasn't all he pretended to be either. Most of the time, he acted like he knew what it was like to be a man. Then, he said he wanted to sleep with Mindy to find what it's like. Dad used his job to hide behind his feelings of being a coward too, according to Mom.

I just hid within myself, Jan suddenly realized. I never told anyone about being bullied. Not even Steve. I was afraid to tell anyone. I thought they'd hassle me about not fighting back. Then, everyone would call me a sissy. So, I pretended nothing was bothering me either. That's how I tried to show toughness. Pastor Enoch said men were always trying to prove they were men. They didn't realize God made them men when he formed them. So, did all guys do this? Are we all pretending to be tough on the outside to hide the fact we are all searching for our own masculinity on the inside?

Jan walked over to his dresser. He opened the sock drawer. Reaching in, his hand pulled out the old baseball. He tossed it up in the air a couple of times and then stared at it in his palm. The situation between him and Mark had not been all Mark's fault, even though Jan liked to think so. Mark did have one reason to be mad at him. Bending his knees, Jan knelt beside his bed and folded his hands. First, he prayed for God to forgive him.

* * * * *

The next day when Jan arrived at the high school, Mr. Guideron motioned him to come into his office. He closed the door as Jan stepped in.

"Hi, Jan. I just wanted to check with you about how everything has been going."

"Good," he said, looking Mr. Guideron in the eyes.

"Your teachers are all indicating you are doing very well grade-wise. Even Coach Ferglund says your attitude toward gym class has changed."

Jan smiled sheepishly.

"How is everything going with Mark Fury?"

"Okay so far."

"No more incidents in hallways or threats to harm you?"

"No, sir. It's been kind of surprising. You know, I was kind of thinking maybe I should talk with Mark."

"About what?"

"I want to see if I can work things out with him. That way we wouldn't have to worry about these problems anymore."

"Are you sure you want to do that?"

"Yes, sir. It would be the right thing to do."

"Do you want me to go with you when you talk to him?"

"No. I need to do this on my own."

"Okay. Well, I wish you the best, Jan. This is very big of you."

"Thank you."

"Well, that's all I needed to see you about. I just wanted to make sure there weren't any more problems."

"Nope," Jan said looking at the school counselor.

Mr. Guideron reached over onto his desk and grabbed a small pad of paper. His scribbled some words down on it and handed it to Jan. "The bell is about to ring. This will get you into class without a problem."

"Thanks," Jan responded as he took the pass. Then he turned around and left the office.

Classes of Modern U.S. History and Biology went well and surprisingly quickly that morning. Jan spent most of his time in gym class lifting weights again to increase his bench press lifts. He also learned his turn to rappel was coming up in a couple of days.

During class time, Mark Fury didn't even make eye contact. It was as though Jan no longer existed. Jan wasn't sure what that meant. Maybe he should just leave the situation with Mark alone. Then he could just toss the baseball into Mark's yard some night. No, that didn't seem like the Christian thing to do. Or even a manly thing to do. Surely, God would want Jan to return the baseball in person and apologize. But how would Mark respond? There was no way of telling.

Jan trudged back to the lunchroom as he thought it over. Making his way through the lunch line, he grabbed a prepackaged pizza slice, a chocolate wafer cookie, and some milk. Next, he looked around the lunchroom. Where to sit? He saw some empty seats back in a far corner. As he made his way toward them, he walked by Barry and noticed the seat next to him was empty. Jan stopped. He glanced at the table in the far corner. The lonely table. Then, he looked back at the seat next to Barry. Barry sat with some of the guys who had been in the locker room the previous day, when they had discussed Mark's scars. Some of the other guys around him could be rather rough characters though. He looked again at the far table. He really did not want to be alone. Jan turned and sat down beside Barry.

"Hey, Jan," Barry noted.

Jan smiled.

One by one, other guys glanced at Jan acceptingly. The biggest of the rough guys looked over at Jan also. The big guy's eyebrows furled briefly. He looked back down at his food and smiled.

"Richards, you're not sitting down with girls today?"

Jan glanced down at the cellophane his hands were ripping off the pizza slice. Then, an odd thought struck him out of nowhere.

"No, Why? Are you afraid of them? I could introduce you," Jan said with a grin.

The guys from the locker room all broke out in laughter.

"Good one, Jan," said Barry.

The big guy shook his head with a grin. Then, he looked up at Jan and nodded in approval.

"Good come-back, Richards," the big guy agreed.

"Hey, you ought to see Jan on that weight machine these days," said Rocky Lyons from gym class.

"One of these days, he may just whip your butt."

"Should I be scared, Richards?"

"You just never know," Jan answered jokingly.

The big guy laughed. Everyone around them seemed to smile at Jan and chuckle a little. Jan relaxed his shoulders and took a bite of pizza.

Chapter 17

When Jan hopped off the bus at the middle school, he decided to head up Spruce Street toward the church. Birds sang and Jan enjoyed the warm breeze as he walked. He didn't know Pastor Enoch's schedule, but he hoped he would be at the church.

To his relief, he saw Pastor in his office as he walked in. Pastor Enoch looked up.

"Hello, Jan. Looking for another project?"

"Sure. I'd work with you again any time."

"Well, let me give that some thought. I can't turn down an offer coming from my right-hand man."

Jan laughed. "Actually, I wanted to talk to you about something else."

"Sure," Pastor said, maneuvering his wheelchair out from behind his desk and coming over to be with Jan. "What's up?"

"I have what you might call a hypothetical problem. Suppose there were these two guys. One committed a sin against the second. The second guy got mad and sinned against the first guy. Then, the first guy kept sinning against the second guy, but the second decided not to sin against the first any longer."

"Okay. I got you so far, Jan."

"The second guy wants to apologize to the first guy and end it. But, the first guy is a very angry person. The second guy doesn't know if the first guy will accept his apology or get mad and hit him."

"That's a tough one, Jan. I would suggest the second guy takes a third person along with him to prevent any violence from happening."

"No, the second guy doesn't want to bring anyone else into the situation. He feels strongly he needs to do it himself."

"I see. Well, I would suggest the second man go to the first man very humbly and apologize for his role in the situation. If the first man doesn't also want to apologize, then the second man should just leave it at that. Some people in this world won't own up their responsibility. The second man needs to be ready to just accept that."

"What if the first guy starts hitting the second guy. The Bible says to turn the other cheek, right?"

"Jan, that is perhaps one of the most misunderstood verses in Scripture. In biblical times, when a man struck another man on the cheek, he was insulting him. So, what Jesus was saying was we don't have to insult him back. It was not about fighting."

"Really?"

"Yes. Jesus lived on Earth during very violent times. The Roman government which ruled over the land allowed soldiers to basically do what they wanted. Roman soldiers would steal things from the Jewish people. People were filled with anger because of that. Naturally, the Jews response was to fight back.

"Jesus wanted to show the people there were other ways to handle these situations. Someone stealing your coat is not more important than human life. A coat is really not worth fighting over when a Roman guard is willing to kill you for it. Just because someone strikes you, doesn't mean you have to strike them back. Be the bigger person. Show them God's love."

"So, what if someone starts hitting you?"

"God gave people the right to protect themselves and their families back in the Old Testament. A Christian can fight back if they feel there is a threat to their health or life, or someone else's. However, we need to be aware of what God would want us to do at that moment. Do you need to protect yourself because the other person is full of rage and won't listen to reason? Or is there something God wants to show the other person by you not fighting back?"

"Wow. That's more complicated than I was expecting."

"Well, let's say it this way: You have the right to protect yourself, Jan. Go with that in mind. If God sends you a feeling not to fight, or if He … uh …"

"Speaks to you in a voice, like in your head," Jan finished.

"A still, small voice?"

Jan nodded.

"Jan, did God …?"

"Yeah. I heard it. Just one sentence. He told me I was His man."

"You sure are, Jan. Remember that. You are a man of God. That is a blessing."

"Guess I should get going."

"One more thing, Jan. Remember, 'We know that for those who love God all things work together for good, for those who are called according to his purpose.' God is already there with you in this situation. Somehow, this figures into His plan for your life. So, you can go in peace."

Pastor Enoch then offered up a prayer for Jan before he left.

After that, Jan wandered around town for a while, sorting through his thoughts. When he finally arrived home, the newspaper had already been delivered. He grabbed it, went into the house and flopped it down in the kitchen table. All stood quiet. Obviously, Sue was off somewhere with friends.

Strolling into his bedroom, Jan dropped his books on his desk and flopped down on his bed, back first. He reached over and took the baseball off his nightstand. As he studied the stitched cowhide, his mind continued to go back to the need to return it to Mark Fury and apologize. When should he do it? It would take all the bravery he had to go there.

The more he thought about it, the less sure he felt about doing it. Would apologizing to Mark really change anything? Suppose he did start a fight there on the spot. Then what? Jan would need to be prepared to stay calm no matter what happened. He had never fought anyone before. Would he even know what to do if that happened? It seemed like it was going to take time to prepare for this. Maybe he should do it tomorrow.

His thoughts were suddenly interrupted by the opening and closing of the outside door. He glanced over at his alarm clock. It didn't even show 5 o'clock yet. Sue? He got up and walked into the kitchen, still carrying the baseball. There stood his mom with a serious look on her face, taking some deep puffs on her cigarette.

"You're home early, Mom."

"Yeah, honey. They let us go early at the plant today. The company has been sold to a larger corporation."

"What?"

"It's okay. We'll just be getting our checks from a different source now. I feel a little sorry for Eleanor Fury though. They fired her."

"Mrs. Fury?"

"Yes. She was not happy when we were leaving."

Jan walked over to the door and peered through its window down the street. He didn't see a car at the Furys' house yet.

"Do you think she's going straight home?"

"No, I saw her and a couple of the other girls pull in to the parking lot at the Big Chief Lounge. I wouldn't want to be near her when she comes out. Why, honey?"

Jan's mind went whirling. Should he tell her? If Mark's mother came home angry and plastered, what would that mean for Mark? How bad might the beating be this time? But what if he was wrong? There was no proof Mark had been beaten. What if he really did beat up other kids? Imagine Mark's anger if he turned Mark's mom in for child abuse?

"Jan? What wrong?"

"I'm not sure. I'm not sure anything is wrong. But it might be."

"Jan, talk to me." His mother stared into his eyes.

"I don't know …." He turned away briefly.

"Jan," his mom said more forcefully.

"Mark comes to school with scars. He's always bragging he beat up on other guys. But no one else comes to school bruised up. The guys think he's lying."

"What are you trying to say?"

"I think maybe his mom beats him. But I don't know for sure."

"What makes you think it's his mom?"

"Once when we were young, his mom yelled at him to come inside the house. When he came out, part of his face looked purple. He took out his anger on me. So, I thought I had done something wrong. Mom, if she comes home drunk and angry, I'm afraid she might …."

Mom took another long drag off her cigarette, looked up at the ceiling and exhaled.

"Well, this puts us in a tough spot, doesn't it," she said, trying to think.

"What do we do?"

"Good question. We don't have absolute proof of this. But, Mark might be in danger."

She thought for a couple of minutes. Then, she said, "Tell you what, let me call your dad's old friend, Sheriff Wilcox. He might be able to give us advice."

Jan felt anxious. He wanted to go and do something. It didn't seem right to just stand there. He looked out the window. Still no car in the drive yet. His fists tightened. Or, at least, he tightened one. The other still held the baseball. The baseball he needed to give back to Mark.

Jan walked over to his mom who was talking on the phone and said in a loud whisper, "Mom, I've got to do something. I'll be right back."

Jan saw her frown but left before she could say anything. Down the street, he ran, holding firmly to the baseball. He had thought over what he might say to Mark when he returned it. This situation,

157

however, added a new dimension to this. How do you tell a guy you know his mom beats him up and tonight she is coming home angry and drunk?

He began to pray. God, tell me what to say. I don't know what I am doing. I need you to be my third person when I talk to Mark. Tell me what to do. His prayer ended as he came to the immaculate steppingstones leading up to the front door of Mark's house.

Neat little rows of flowers were budding along the sides of the steppingstones. In summer, they had one of the most beautiful lawns in town. And inside, a woman beat her son. It didn't seem possible. It didn't make sense. What if he was wrong about Mark's mom?

Jan came to a complete stop. The house stood about 15 feet away. Buckets of flowers would be hanging from the porch soon. All kinds of beautiful colors would soon be making a little frame around the dark foundation of the house.

He took a deep breath. What if he was wrong? Could something so evil as child abuse be going on inside such a beautiful home? She never seemed like that sort of person in public. Yet, her son was very angry, mean, and cruel. What else could be causing that?

"God, be with me," Jan whispered. Breathing deeply again, he began to step upon the steppingstones. Each one brought him closer to the house. It would be easier to just return the baseball and leave. Not even mention Mark's mom. But men protect, as Pastor said. Mark may need protection. Jan had to do this.

His heart racing, Jan looked down at the baseball in his hand one more time. He forced his legs to climb the steps. His soul stood tall inside.

"Whatever happens God will make good out of it," he reminded himself in a whisper.

You are my man. Words came back to him again.

With determination, Jan raised his arm and brought his fist down on the door three times. Within, he could hear some kind of movement. Then, footsteps came closer. The only other sound was Jan's breathing. A click came from the doorknob. The door slowly opened.

Mark Fury peeked through the crack in the door. At least, he looked like Mark Fury. There was a façade of toughness on his face, but it seemed very shallow. Mark's face looked pale and the eyebrows usually knitted together in a frown were now loose and being pulled upward.

"Yeah," he said.

Jan swallowed. "Mark, I just wanted to return this," He showed him the baseball. "I took it from you a long time ago, and I'm sorry. That was wrong."

Mark seemed in a state of shock, trying to interpret the meaning of Jan's words. His eyes darted to the street corner.

"Okay," Mark said with a total absence of emotion.

Jan paused, looking down, as he gathered his next words.

"My … uh … my mom told me your mom got fired today. She said she was very angry and went to the bar."

Jan looked into Mark's eyes. They made contact. The whole façade of toughness fell away now. Any anger seemed totally absent from his face, replaced by a hint of something else. Fear?

"Do you want to … come over to my place for a while?"

As soon as the words left Jan's mouth, they both heard the sound of rubber rolling to a stop on pavement just down the street. Their heads turned and they saw Mark's mom's car make the turn onto Ithaca Street from Park Street, heading in their direction. It wobbled a little, trying to find the correct lane. The figure inside seemed to have difficulty sitting up straight as she rounded the corner.

Jan turned back to Mark. "You can come to my place."

Mark glanced at the approaching car and then back to Jan. He looked deeply into Jan's eyes, as if trying to pull out whatever information Jan had. I know, Jan thought loudly in his head. I know. Both turned again as the car passed by the front of the house and began its turn toward the driveway. Mrs. Fury stared at them through the car window, with a familiar look. It was the look Mark usually had before he did something cruel to Jan. Narrowed, angry eyes.

"I know … what she does" Jan whispered loudly. "Let's go." Jan

159

handed the baseball back to Mark.

Mark stared at it for a moment as if trying to remember its significance. They heard the car door open on the other side of the house. Then came a couple of groans and some cussing. Jan looked at Mark who stood unmoving in his place, looking wide-eyed at the corner of the house.

"Come on," Jan whispered loudly again. Then, in an awkward gesture, Jan grabbed ahold of Mark's hand, the one with the baseball in it, and pulled with every ounce of strength his skinny arms had. Mark burst from the door as Jan dashed down the steps. Out into Ithaca Street, they ran, Jan holding onto Mark's hand, with the baseball still in it, and dragging him behind. Clomp! Clomp! Clomp! Their tennis shoes made loud noises as they ran on the purplish pavement. Mark just stared ahead, trying to keep up with Jan, but showing very little effort of his own to go forward. They passed three houses and then crossed Park Street. The young men dashed passed a corner house and an old church building, now used as a karate club.

Finally, they careened off the street and jogged into Jan's yard. They slowed down, taking the last of their final giant steps. Mark, beginning to show signs of thought again, yanked his hand from Jan's. The baseball dropped onto the lawn with a dull thud. Jan looked down at it.

"You can have it," Mark said, trying to catch his breath and rubbing his palm against his jeans.

Also panting, Jan looked at his own palm and did likewise.

The door to Jan's house sprang open and his mom called out. "Get in here, both of you."

She stared down Ithaca Street behind them. The boys turned. Totally bombed, Mrs. Fury trudged down the street toward them, weaving in and out of some imaginary line she couldn't quite see. As the boys passed by Jan's mother, they saw the phone in her hand, with the cord pulled tight from the wall.

"Yup. That's her coming down the street now toward our house. Drunk as a skunk," Jan's mom said into the phone. "Okay. See you in a few minutes."

She hung up the phone and turned to look at the boys. She grabbed the newspaper from the kitchen table and handed it to Jan. "You go into Jan's room and do some reading or something. I'll handle this."

The determination in her face now was something Jan had not seen in years. Not since the accident.

Together, they went through the living room into Jan's bedroom and closed the door behind them. They both plopped down on the shag carpet floor, resting their backs against the side of Jan's bed and breathed out a sigh of relief. Following orders, Jan nervously ran his fingers through the newspaper sections. He grabbed one out and handed it to Mark.

"Sports?" Jan offered.

"Nah," Mark said. "Have you got the comics?"

A huge grin crossed Jan's face as he dropped the sports pages and grabbed the section with the comics in it. As Jan passed it over, Mark snatched it up.

"I didn't know you liked comics," said Jan.

"How else would I know Brenda Starr?" Mark asked, giving a little smile.

Their eyes stared at newspaper pages as they heard a knock on the outside door. But their ears listened intently for sounds from the kitchen.

They heard the door opened.

"Hello, Eleanor," Jan's mom said calmly.

"I think … I think … my son is here," said Mrs. Fury, slurring her words. "It's dinner time … and he needs to … come home … with me."

"You don't look like you're in very good condition, Eleanor. Why don't you go home and rest a little bit? I'll send Mark back after we eat."

All right, Mom! thought Jan. Her patience and calmness were amazing.

Then came a long silence. Jan and Mark looked at each other, holding their breath.

"No ... I really want him ... to come home ... with me."

"I don't think that's a good idea, Eleanor. You look like you need some rest."

"You're trying ... to get back at me, ... aren't you?" said Mrs. Fury angrily and louder, still slurring her words.

Mark looked back down at the comics section and rubbed his forehead.

"Eleanor, I don't have a reason to get back at you. Now, go home and get some sleep." Jan's mom remained calm.

Mrs. Fury cussed at her. "You took my man and now ... you want my son, ... don't you?"

Jan looked up at the ceiling now. Did Mark know about any of this? And how much? Mrs. Fury sounded even angrier. How much farther would she push about their teenage rivalry?

"Eleanor, you need to go home now. This has nothing to do with our years in school together."

More cuss words tumbled off Mrs. Fury's tongue. "Get out of my way. I am taking that no-good son of mine."

Jan jumped to his feet, his fists cocked. He had always been told by his dad never to hit a woman. Pastor's Enoch's words about treating women with gentleness and kindness came back to him. So, he wasn't sure what he would do if Mrs. Fury made her way to his bedroom door.

Mark stood up frustrated. "I'd better go with her. She'll cause more trouble."

"No," said Jan firmly. He held his arm out to prevent Mark from getting any closer to the door.

In the kitchen, they heard a bit of scuffling.

"Eleanor, I did not invite you in here. Stay out."

"You can't hold my son ... from me, Marge. That's kidnapping."

Kidnapping? thought Jan. They were protecting Mark. How could he and his mom get in trouble for kidnapping?

"Okay, Eleanor, settle down. I'll let you see him." She paused just briefly. "Jan, can you have Mark come out, please?"

Mark began to move forward, but again Jan held him back with his arm.

"Let me go first," Jan said quietly.

Mark sighed but nodded. Jan placed his hand on the doorknob and turned. The door opened inward, revealing the blue living room. Jan looked around the corner to the right. Through the doorway into the kitchen, between the pink cupboards and the countertop, he could just barely see his mom's back as she stood in the mudroom, her arms holding tightly to the outside door frame. On the other side of the doorway, Mrs. Fury was pressed up against his mom's left arm, attempting to see in.

Slowly, Jan made his way into the kitchen, keeping Mark behind him. Mrs. Fury looked straight at her son.

"Mark! It's time to come home," she shouted.

"He's going to stay with us for a little longer," said Jan loudly. "He and I are talking."

"Shut up, you … scrawny, little excuse … for a man," ordered Mrs. Fury. She pressed harder against his mom's forearm. Mom held her position, braced the bottoms of her feet to the mudroom linoleum.

Sissy-boy.

The negative voice pricked Jan's heart. Still, he stood firm. He ordered his soul to do likewise. God, we need you, he thought.

"You shut up, Mom!" Mark yelled out suddenly.

"You dare to show me disrespect? You puny little …." Mrs. Fury's eyes were red and watery, filled with anger. "I wished I'd aborted you when I had the chance."

"And I wish you weren't my mother either," Mark shouted back.

She threw herself now at Jan's mom's arm. Her arm reached out, wanting to grab onto her son. Jan's mom's feet slid a little, but her arms held strong.

"Eleanor, please, go home," said his mom forcefully but still calm.

Mrs. Fury drew her right arm back, her palm prepared to strike. Then, before it could come forward to do damage, a hand grabbed her wrist from behind and held tight. She turned in raging anger to see who was behind her.

"This is enough, Eleanor," came Sheriff Wilcox's gravelly voice. "What are people going to say if they find out you've been arrested? Imagine what that will do to your family's name. What would your father say?"

"They fired me, Hank," Mrs. Fury cried out. Suddenly, the anger seemed to pass out of her. Her head came to rest on the sheriff's shoulder and she began sobbing. "People keep taking things away from me. It's not fair."

The sheriff guided her down the porch steps. "Now, Eleanor, we're gonna go back to your house and talk about this. Just you and me. Mark is gonna stay here with Marge and her son 'til I come back, okay?"

Mrs. Fury's only reply was more sobbing as he guided her over to his patrol car.

Chapter 18

On July fourth, Jan awoke to a cool breeze across his body from the fan in the window. He had kicked all the covers off during the night, attempting to keep cool. Sheets beneath him were soaked from sweat. The bicentennial of the nation's day of independence had finally arrived. Today would be a full day.

There would be the traditional parade at 12:30, followed by a water hose battle between two local fire departments. There would be free slices of watermelon being passed out at the A&P store. One of main events was the traditional greased pole in the city park. Participants would try to cross the AuSable River in the city park by venturing across a long greased pole without falling off and into the water a few feet below.

Various other businesses in town were all finding their own ways to celebrate America's 200th birthday. The Mercantile had been selling patriotic colored clothing since spring. Bob's Drive-In was offering bicentennial parfaits with cherries and miniature '76 flag for only 75 cents. Even if those weren't appealing, they still sold ice cream and burgers. Jan usually visited them for their giant 32-ounce shakes.

It was hard to believe the school year had been over for a few weeks already. No more gym class. Although, the class had ended on a positive note there. With help from Barry, Jan had been successful at rappelling from the platform near the gym ceiling. By the end of class, he had achieved a B- for his effort, the highest score he would ever get in gym. His fear of shower rooms had also vanished once he realized they were all just guys, even with their differences.

Jan had managed to keep his grades up in his other classes for the rest of the semester. Thankfully, his intestinal episodes had been less common. They still occurred occasionally but no longer lasted for over a week, causing him to miss several days of school at a time. In Public Speaking class, he gave his final speech on his father and his achievements during World War II. His mom had helped him research the information. For Biology, Jan had been in a dissecting group with one of the girls who loved hunting. So, he didn't have to worry about cutting open the frog. Borderlines of Reality and drawing class were natural As on his report card.

During the first couple weeks which had followed Sheriff Wilcox's confrontation with Mrs. Fury at their house, the situations at both the Fury and Richards's households felt a little awkward. When Jan and his mom would run into the Furys while out and about around town, however, they smiled at each other and said hello. No mention of the incident with the sheriff was ever made again. Local social workers met with Mrs. Fury and Mark regularly. Sue, as was typical for her, remained so focused on the unfairness in society, she never did find out what happened at their house that day. Especially what a hero her mom had been.

The relationship between Jan and Mark had flipped over like a coin. No more bullying. In fact, sometimes they ate together at lunch and talked about what was happening in various newspaper comics. Jan shared with Mark all his dad had told him about the different strips. It was as if, instead of being enemies for all those years, they had been friends – as if the baseball incident hadn't even happened.

As for Weasel, he had been suspended from school for two weeks after his attempt to steal that boy's lunch money. From then on, he kept his distance from Jan and no longer even made eye contact with him. All that change in Weasel just because Jan's pushed him down while trying to help protect a little boy.

Steve's parents were not happy to learn about Mindy's pregnancy. Both sets of parents agreed to have Mindy attend a home for unwed mothers on the west side of the state until the baby was born. Then, they placed the baby up for adoption.

Steve had to hand over the money he had been saving for his used car to his parents. It would now go toward Mindy's stay at the home. He would also not be able to drive the family station wagon anywhere without them until the second semester of his junior year. Even worse, he would not be allowed to buy his own car until after graduation. His dad stopped going to the bar on a regular basis, too, after learning of the pregnancy scare. Maybe some good was coming out of all that had happened.

Steve did manage to pull up his courage and tell Jenny about the situation with Mindy. Despite his wandering eyes, Steve took his responsibility seriously. Of course, Jenny broke up with him on the spot. Ever since, he had been trying to win her back, but his suave, confident manner had been replaced with more humility. Supposedly, Steve had talked Jenny into watching the fireworks together tonight. They invited Jan to sit with them.

Jan might do that, but there would be a change this time. Toward the end of the year, a new girl had moved to Gunwale. Her name was Darcy. She was also a sophomore and had dark, curly hair and glasses. Not very tall, she was full of energy and loved cross country running. In fact, Jan had met her on the trails along the river, where she liked to run. They seemed to hit it off. So, Jan had asked her to watch the fireworks with him. Maybe they would sit with Steve and Jenny, but maybe they wouldn't. Jan wasn't quite sure.

Putting on his bathrobe, he stepped out into the living room. The house stood quiet. Neither his mom nor Sue were up yet. It was Sunday. So, they wouldn't be in bed for too long. He walked over and looked into the trophy case. Amid his dad's trophies, in the space once empty sat a thank-you card. It was made out to Jan and had come from Pastor Enoch and the congregation in thanks for his service in building the bookshelves.

He turned. A pile of newspapers lay in a weaved basket beside his mom's tan recliner. He had almost forgotten, the Sunday edition would be out this morning with its comics section in full color. All his favorite comic strips had started new adventures now. Brenda Starr and her husband had returned from their honeymoon safe and sound. Detective Dick Tracy had closed the case on Lispy and her new partner Pucker Puss, ending their crime spree. The Phantom had returned the Star of Bangalla to its rightful owner. Dondi had begun a new adventure as well. Life in the comic world continued.

As Jan thought about his day, he realized how busy it would be. He might have to wait until after the fireworks to read the comics. But that was okay. They'd be waiting for him.

Jan walked back into his bedroom and began preparing his church clothes. He might as well take advantage of the quiet in the house for the moment and take his shower now. As he laid his clothes out on his bed, he glanced over at the nightstand.

Now, along with his Bible, the three by five card and a Phantom comic book, a baseball rested on top. There was an irony there. The baseball used to remain hidden, a symbol of his shame. Since the transformation in his relationship with Mark, it stood for something else. Friendship maybe? No. More than that. Maybe bravery. Yet that didn't seem to cover its new meaning either. Whatever the new meaning was, the baseball proudly sat beside him on his nightstand every night, reminding him of everything he had been through and how God had suddenly changed it all before his eyes.

Jan smiled, scooped up his clothes and headed for the bathroom. God was waiting.

Study Questions

Prologue

1. Bravery is an important attribute, especially for men. Many times in Scripture, God tells His people to "be brave." When you read of God telling someone to be "be brave," do you hear it as a gentle, encouraging voice or as an angry, threatening voice? Which way do you think Jan hears it?

2. The fears in Jan's life are not just of bullies. He also seems to fear his father and God in some ways. Why is that?

Chapter One

1. Jan is concerned about his physical development because he seems to be developing slower than his classmates. How important is physical appearance in general to young teens?

2. Toughness is another manly attribute noted in Chapter One. What does being tough mean? Was Jesus tough? In what way?

Chapter Two

1. Throughout the beginning of this chapter, Jan sees students engaged in activities which might or might not be considered bullying. What determines if an action is bullying or not? How might these behaviors affect a bullying victim as opposed to someone who hasn't been bullied much?

2. In Matthew 5:22, Jesus speaks out against name calling. Jan, like many guys, is hurt by words attacking his masculinity. What do you think Jesus would have to say about verbal attacks on someone's gender? As His followers, how should we view this behavior?

Chapter Three

1. Jan appears to be keeping his bullying situation a secret from everyone. However, we know the stress is getting to him. What could happen when a teen keeps such strong emotions locked up inside of him?

2. In the rest room, Mark Fury attacks Jan verbally in the most harmful way he knows how and even threatens violence against him. What do you think this is doing to Jan's already shaky sense of self-worth and sense of masculinity? How important is a sense of masculinity to a boy this age?

Chapter Four

1. When Jan returns home after his rough day at school, we learn about two of his hobbies, reading comics and drawing. Artists tend to be sensitive individuals, like Jan is. Sensitivity is an important trait in artistic ability, but it also makes the artist vulnerable. Our culture has mixed feelings about men being sensitive. Based upon the Bible's teachings, is sensitivity in men a good trait?

2. Jan's mom's behavior towards him has changed drastically from the prologue of this story. Why do you think this has happened? What do you think of her new way of treating Jan?

Chapter Five

1. In Chapter Five, Jan's thoughts about the comic book story on bullying and instruction from a Sunday school teacher really sum

2. up the struggle within him. In Exodus 22:2, God tells men they have a right to protect their family and possessions from someone breaking into their house. However, in Matthew 5, Jesus talks about loving your neighbor and not hitting back when someone strikes you. How do these verses impact the topic of bullying? Does fighting to protect your body from harm violate what Jesus said in Matthew 5:22?

Chapter Six

1. Gym class once again causes Jan to ponder his place in the male hierarchy at school. In the early teen years, boys are often wowed by guys who develop early, who have chest hairs, large muscles and so on. A lot of importance is placed on the physical attributes. Now, read 1 Samuel 13:1-13. What does God says about these?
2. At the end of the chapter, while Jan is showering, he hears other boys laughing out by the lockers. He assumes they are laughing about him but doesn't know for sure. Can bullying affect a person's perception of other people? Why would that be?

Chapter Seven

1. Jan walks down to the church after school to help the pastor. Although the pastor seems kind, Jan is still frightened about helping him with a project. Why? What does he fear will happen?
2. In this chapter we meet Jan's other bully, Weasel Birler. How is Weasel different from Mark Fury in the way he bullies Jan?

Chapter Eight

1. What is Pastor Enoch's view on the part shame plays in our lives?

2. This is the first time we see Jan begin to open up about his concerns in any way. Why is that?

Chapter Nine

1. The conflict between Jan and Mark escalates in this chapter. However, Mark likes to keep the adults in the dark as to what he is doing. How does he present himself to the school bus driver and the coach?
2. Jan avoids a fight with Mark this time. Yet, without Mark even saying a word, we can tell their showdown has only been delayed. Why?

Chapter Ten

1. The school principal and counselor both become involved in Jan and Mark's situation. We would hope it would now be resolved in Jan's favor. What happens?
2. How do you think Principal Stone's words to Mr. Guideron will impact Jan?

Chapter Eleven

1. This finally reveals what the title of the book means. Explain Pastor Enoch's theory about every man's greatest fear.
2. What affect does this session between the two have on each one?

Chapter Twelve

1. Once again Jan faces Weasel. What differences do you notice between the way Weasel bullies Jan and the way Mark Fury does? What might motivate Weasel to bully others?
2. Back at home, Jan faces his toughest mental battle with the

negative voice. It attacks him mercilessly. Jan looks to God to save him. However, God does not answer. Or does He?

Chapter Thirteen

1. How do Jan and Mark's understanding of the opposite sex differ?
2. Describe how Jan's life is suddenly changed the next morning by his own reflection and a new voice and how this event transforms his perception in gym class.

Chapter Fourteen

1. How is Jan now seeing recent events? How do they fit a pattern?
2. Describe how Jan's talk with his mom impacts his understanding about both of his parents and his relationship with his mom.

Chapter Fifteen

1. In what ways does Pastor Enoch see men and women differently?
2. How are circumstances different when Jan faces the Weasel again?
3. BONUS: Name the famous gymnast at the 1976 Olympics who really did march into the gym and dance away with the medals?

Chapter Sixteen

1. The other guys in the locker room begin to doubt Mark's stories of fighting other kids. Why?
2. What is the secret of the baseball?

Chapter Seventeen

1. Jan makes a decision which will take all the bravery he can find to fulfill. Talk about that.
2. The relationship changes between Jan and Mark when circumstances take them in an unexpected direction. How does this affect them?

Chapter Eighteen

1. In what ways is Jan's life now different than at the beginning of the book?
2. The negative voice plays an important role in Jan's life. Do you think it is a mental health issue or something else?

Bible Verse References by Theme

DESIGNED BY GOD FOR A PURPOSE
Jeremiah 1:4-5; Psalms 139:13-14; Exodus 4:11-12; Ephesians 2:10

SHAME
Genesis 2:25; Genesis 3:7; Psalm 44:15; Psalm 13; 1 Peter 2:6

SIN & SALVATION
Romans 3:10; Romans 3:23; Romans 5:12; Romans 6:23; Romans 5:8-9; Romans 10:9-10;
Romans 10:13

BEHAVIOR
1 Thessalonians 4:11; Hebrews 12:14; Colossians 3:5; Philippians 4:8

BRAVERY/COURAGE
Joshua 1:9; Deuteronomy 3:22; Joshua 23:6; 1 Corinthians 16:13

TREATMENT OF WOMEN
Ephesians 5:25; Ephesians 5:28; Colossians 3:19

THE ARTS
Exodus 31:1-5

GLOSSARY

Prologue
six-shooter — a pistol used in the wild West which shot only six bullets at a time before needing to be reloaded
Chapter One
plod — to walk slowly with heavy steps
Chapter Two
spinster — slang and offensive term for a woman who never married
cesspool — a pit for retaining sewage
Chapter Four
zealous — seriously devoted to a cause
Chapter Five
parapets — an elevated feature raised above the main wall of a castle or old church
Chapter Six
ruddy — reddish in color
Tenebrae service — a church service with very low lighting to create a sad and serious atmosphere
chancel — the space around the altar at the front of a church sanctuary
narthex — fellowship area of a church
chauvinist — a person who believes one gender is superior to another
Don Juan — the name of a famous Spanish nobleman who was a womanizer
belting - hitting someone hard with a fist
Chapter Seven
debasing — reducing something or someone in value or significance
Chapter Eight
war orphan — a child left without parents because of a war
Chapter Nine

stump-jumping – cruising down old two-track roads through the woods

duke it out — slang term for fistfight

frenzy – a fit or spell of extreme agitation or violence

Chapter Ten

on the lam — slang term for hiding out, keeping out of sight

Chapter Eleven

invulnerable – incapable of being wounded, hurt, or damaged.

sawhorses — a beam with four legs used to support a board or plank for sawing

Chapter Thirteen

mezzanine – balcony of a gym

Chapter Fourteen

concocted – created

Manasseh – the Israelite tribe descended from Joseph in the Old Testament of the Bible

Chapter Fifteen

Sabbath – a day rest declared by God in the Bible

booked – slang term for ran fast

COMIC STRIP GLOSSARY

Brenda Starr, Reporter *(1940-2011)* was one of the few newspaper comics created by a woman. Her world-spanning adventures inspired many young women to become journalists. (TM and © Tribune Media Content)

Connie *(1927 to 1941)* was an American adventure comic strip featuring Connie Kurridge, a "modern" young woman whose occupations included aviator, charity worker, reporter and detective. (© Ledger Syndicate)

Dick Tracy *(1931-present)* was inspired by police's battle against organized crime, especially in the Chicago area. His comic paved the way for the more serious comics of the 1930s. (TM and © Tribune

Media Content; *www.gocomics.com/dicktracy/*)

Dondi *(1955-1986)* was about a war orphan who made his way to America where he was adopted. The strip was a mixture of family drama and boy adventures with his gang, the Explorers Club. (© Tribune Media Content)

Gasoline Alley *(1918-present)* features the humorous life of a small town family, the Wallets, and their friends, including Miss Melba, throughout the decades. (TM and © Tribune Media Content; *www.gocomics.com/gasoline alley*)

Joe Palooka *(1930-1984)* was a kind-hearted champion boxer who traveled the world, not only battling other boxers, but criminals as well and helping those in need. (© McNaught Syndicate)

Mary Worth *(1938-present)* is a soap opera strip about people in an apartment complex who seek the wisdom of neighbor, Mary Worth, when in trouble. (TM and © King Features Syndicate; *www.comicskingdom.com/mary-worth*)

The Phantom *(1936-present)* was the first costumed

hero in comics. He paved the way for Superman, Batman and others we have today.(TM and © King Features Syndicate; *www.comicskingdom.com/phantom*)

Popeye *(1929-present)* first appeared in a comic called "Thimble Theater" starring Olive Oyl and her family. He quickly became the star. His adventures against his adversary Bluto have been featured in cartoons, movies and comics. (TM and © King Features Syndicate; *www.comicskingdom.com/popeye*)

Tilly the Toiler *(1921-1959)* was a humor strip about a career girl who worked for fashionable women's wear company. Her initiative at work became the source of innovation and humor. (© King Features Syndicate)

My Plan against Bullying

After reading through this book, you can use its information and your own thoughts to create a plan for yourself to handle bullying.

1. Adults I can trust to talk to if I am being bullied …

_____

_____

_____

_____

2. The best ways for me to avoid a bully are …

_____

_____

_____

_____

3. When a bully is bothering me, I feel …
____Hurt____Scared____Sad____Angry
____Ashamed of myself____ Confused

4. What hurts most is when a bully …

_____

_____

_____

_____

5. If I am feeling hopeless about a bullying situation, I will …

_____

_____

_____

6. If I see someone else being bullied at school, I will ...

_____

_____

_____

_____

7. If I see someone else being bullied outside of school, I will ...

_____

_____

_____

_____

8. If someone tells me they are being bullied I can ...

_____

_____

_____

_____

REMINDER CARD

God designed me

For you formed my inward parts;

you knitted me together in my mother's womb.

I praise you, for I am fearfully and wonderfully made.

Wonderful are your works;

my soul knows it very well. (Psalm 139:13-15)

He even created the parts I don't like or understand their purpose

Then the Lord said to him, "Who has made man's mouth? Who makes him mute, or deaf, or seeing, or blind? Is it not I, the Lord? Now therefore go, and I will be with your mouth and teach you what you shall speak." (Exodus 4:11-12)

He designed me to fulfill a purpose in His greater plan.

For we are his workmanship, created in Christ Jesus for good works, which God prepared beforehand, that we should walk in them. (Ephesians 2:10)